A COLLECTION OF SHORT STORIES

GIACOMO GIAMMATTEO

Inferno Publishing Company

Cover design by Natasha Brown

Book design by Giacomo Giammatteo

This edition was prepared by Giacomo Giammatteo gg@giacomog.com

Print ISBN 978-1-949074-76-5

Electronic ISBN 978-1-949074-74-1

❀ Formatted with Vellum

PART ONE

A CASE OF BLINDNESS

A heartwarming drama that explores redemption and understanding amid prejudice. After losing his sight in the War, Grandpa Walker is left bitter and isolated in his modest home. He spends most of his time sitting in his library or rocking on the front porch.

When his grandson, Tony, brings home Shannon — a bright, compassionate student — an unexpected friendship begins. Through shared literature and candid conversation, Grandpa confronts his biases, reconnects with life, and slowly opens his heart to diversity.

Set in a modern household, this touching story champions empathy, growth, and the transformative power of compassion.

A CASE OF BLINDNESS

Shannon always believed that books had the power to bridge seemingly impossible divides. That's what her mother, a literature professor, instilled in her. She said a good story could open anyone's mind. Shannon never realized how true that was until she met Grandpa Walker.

It began with an English project her class had been assigned in school. Shanon was partnered with Tony, and though Tony wasn't an avid reader, Shannon was looking forward to the project. If there was anything she liked more than reading, it was helping other people learn, and Tony seemed to be one who needed it. It wasn't that he couldn't learn; he simply wasn't interested.

The day they got the assignment, they met after school to discuss how to proceed. "We can't go to my house," Shannon said. "My mom wouldn't approve of us being there without supervision. We could go to the library, though."

Tony shrugged. "I guess, but we could also work at my house, but you're gonna have to ignore my grandfather. He's prejudiced as hell – against everybody."

Shannon thought nothing of it. "No problem. I've seen lots of prejudiced people."

But the night before they were to start working together, Shannon got a glimpse of what she'd be facing.

She stopped by Tony's house to drop off some reference materials, and when Tony opened the door, she witnessed an interaction that made her both concerned and more determined than ever.

Tony invited her in, but tiptoed across the foyer toward the kitchen. He peeked around the corner before quietly crossing the room, but he wasn't quiet enough — the floor creaked, causing his grandfather to turn his head sharply.

"About time you got home. Anybody with you?" he asked, his tone suspicious.

Tony looked surprised. He glanced behind him, facing Shannon, then held his fingers to his lips and turned back to his grandfather. "Nobody."

Grandpa sniffed the air. "You smell like garlic. You been hanging out with those damn Italians again?"

Tony sighed and dropped his backpack on a chair. "Marco's mom invited me for dinner. She even sent some lasagna home for you."

"I already ordered food for both of us. Should be here anytime," Grandpa said.

"Thanks, Grandpa, but like I said, I already ate."

"What's that?" Grandpa asked.

"Nothing. I have homework."

"When I was your age, I worked. I didn't waste time with foreigners and their spicy food," Grandpa said.

Tony stood in the doorway, debating whether to engage. "Grandpa, why do you complain about my friends so much? They're good kids. Besides, Marco was born here, and so were his parents."

"Still Italian," Grandpa said.

Tony shook his head and walked toward the kitchen. "I've got a friend coming over to help me study. Would you *please* not do anything to embarrass me?"

"I hope it's not that Jewish kid with the funny hat."

"David wears a yarmulke," Tony said, exasperated, "and no, the person coming over is someone you haven't met."

Shannon stepped toward the door, making sure she was quiet. Now she understood Tony's warnings, but rather than being discouraged, she was even more determined to make a connection.

Tony let Shannon out, and was walking up the stairs when Grandpa yelled something else unintelligible.

"Good night, Grandpa," Tony said firmly, leaving his grandfather alone with his prejudice.

Shannon planned on meeting Tony at his house the next day, and despite Tony's warnings about how old-fashioned and prejudiced his grandfather was, she was eager to accept the challenge.

After school, she went home with Tony to start their project. Before they even stepped through the door, Tony warned her again.

"Be patient, Shannon," Tony whispered as they climbed the steps to a modest two-story home. "He's been a bitter old man ever since he lost his sight during the Vietnam War. And he blames every ethnic group you can think of for what happened."

"Why does he blame ethnic groups?" Shannon asked.

"He said his squad was nothing but foreigners, which meant anything from Irish, to Italian, Latino, or Black. Then he said the ones who shot him were Chinese — even though they were Vietnamese."

Shannon nodded, squeezing her stack of books tighter against her chest. She could handle prejudice — she'd seen it her whole life — but she knew better than to lead with that part of her identity. Sometimes, you need to let people see *who* you are before they can see *what* you are.

They stepped into the living room, which was impeccably clean with floor-to-ceiling bookshelves lining the walls. Shannon moved closer to take a look.

Sitting there, right in front of her, were all the classics, their spines faded but well-cared for. And everything was sparkling clean. Even the shelves were free of dust.

Grandpa Walker sat in a worn armchair, dark glasses covering his eyes, and his posture rigid. His fingers traced the arm of the chair, something he had done so often that the fabric was worn almost to the wood.

As Shannon examined the books, Grandpa's head turned sharply in her direction. Tony spoke before Shannon could.

"Grandpa, this is Shannon. We're partners on an English project."

Grandpa's expression remained guarded. "She gonna be able to help you?"

His comment gave Shannon a chance to make a good impression. "I hope so, Mr. Walker. Tony speaks very highly of you, and I want him to live up to your expectations."

Grandpa's eyebrows rose above the dark glasses. "Speaks highly of me? Does he?"

"He said you used to be an English teacher. And a writer."

"Thirty years at Roosevelt High," he said, warming slightly.

Shannon set her English books on the coffee table and sat in a chair opposite Grandpa. "That's impressive. My mother always said teaching is the noblest profession."

Tony seemed impatient, and he gestured for Shannon to follow him. She stood, and it looked as if she'd follow him, but a certain book caught her eye. She walked back to the bookshelves, a gleeful smile showing on her face. She couldn't help herself.

"Oh my goodness. What a collection!" Shannon ran her fingers lightly along the spines. "Hemingway, Steinbeck, Fitzgerald ..." Then she reached for the one that had caught her eye. "*To Kill a Mockingbird*! I just finished reading this."

She pulled it from the shelf and opened it. "Oh my God! It's a first edition."

"Girl your age reading Harper Lee?" Grandpa said, with a touch of sarcasm. "I doubt that, unless you used CliffNotes?"

"You never really understand a person until you consider things from his point of view ... until you climb into his skin and walk around in it," Shannon quoted, undeterred.

Grandpa's eyebrows shot up. "So you really do read them?"

"Who hasn't?" Shannon replied.

"That a quote from the book?" Tony asked, clearly surprised.

"I have a pretty good memory for things I love," Shannon said.

Then she continued examining the shelves with genuine appreciation, pulling books out and handling them with care.

Then an idea struck her. "Mr. Walker, would you like me to read some of these to you? I know it must be killing you to have all these wonderful books and not be able to read them."

He began to shake his head but stopped. "I haven't read in years, but if you want to try ..."

Tony stared at his grandfather in disbelief.

"How about now?" Shannon suggested. "We have some time before Tony and I need to start our project."

"Well ... I suppose a chapter wouldn't hurt," he said, reluctantly.

Shannon sat near Grandpa and opened *To Kill a Mockingbird*.

Tony, still stunned, backed away. "I'll get some snacks."

As she began to read, Grandpa leaned back, a rare look of contentment crossing his face.

Shannon's words flowed naturally, as if Harper Lee herself was guiding her voice. She felt a connection forming — not just to the story, but to this grumpy old man who seemed to soften with each paragraph.

Over the next week, their routine became established. Shannon came over, supposedly to work with Tony, but spent the first hour reading to Grandpa. With each visit, he grew more relaxed, more welcoming. The rigid posture eased, and occasionally, he even smiled.

"You've got a gift, girl," he said to her one evening after she closed the book. "Voice like a bell."

"Thank you, Mr. Walker."

"Call me Grandpa."

Shannon smiled, touched by the invitation. "Okay, Grandpa."

Tony entered and handed her coat to her. "It's getting late. I should walk you home."

"I'll be back tomorrow, Grandpa. We can read a few more chapters."

His voice showed excitement for the first time. "Maybe more?"

Shannon smiled and touched his shoulder warmly before following Tony toward the door.

What Tony didn't know, what Shannon never told him, was that she heard Grandpa's words after they left. She had forgotten her scarf and turned back just in time to hear him say, "By God, Tony. You finally brought home someone with class. And brains. Girl's smart as a whip."

Shannon felt a pang of guilt. He didn't know who she really was yet. But she was beginning to care for this cantankerous old man, and she knew that when the moment came to reveal herself, it would be painful for both of them.

Two weeks later, they'd settled into a comfortable routine. Shannon read, Grandpa listened, and the prejudice that Tony had warned her about seemed to fade into the background. But she knew it was still there, dormant rather than defeated.

"That's the end of chapter twenty," Shannon said, closing the book. "Do you want to start another one, or wait until tomorrow?"

"We'll wait," he said. "You know, this reminds me why I taught English all those years. I'd like to treasure the memories."

Shannon decided it was time to take their relationship beyond the confines of his living room. "I was thinking, Grandpa ... would you like to go to the park tomorrow? It's supposed to be a beautiful day."

He hesitated. "I don't get out much."

"Fresh air would do you good. Tony can come too."

"Well, I suppose my old bones could use the sun."

"Perfect! I'll bring lunch."

"I don't like many foods."

"Roast beef and cheese with onions and tomatoes? Right?" Shannon asked, remembering what Tony had told her about his grandfather's preferences.

His face displayed shock, then a smile. "How did you know that?"

"We all have secrets, Grandpa," she said, knowing that soon, her own secret would have to be revealed.

The next day was perfect — sunny with a gentle breeze. Shannon guided Grandpa to a bench while Tony followed with a small cooler.

"There's a nice breeze, and the flowers are blooming. Take a whiff, Grandpa. The air smells sweet."

He inhaled deeply and smiled. "It's good to be outside. Thank you, Shannon. It's been too long."

Shannon unpacked the sandwiches and handed one to him. "Roast beef, made to your liking."

An older man walked his beagle along the sidewalk. Tony waved. "Hi, Mr. Leibowitz. How's the pup?"

"That the Jew from down the street? Always letting that mutt do its business on my sidewalk."

Shannon glanced at Tony, her eyes narrowing with concern. "I'm sure he cleans up after his dog, Grandpa."

"That's what they all say."

Nearby, two young Chinese-American boys ran by, laughing and speaking to each other in accented English.

"What's that racket?" Grandpa asked.

Shannon laughed. "Just some kids playing, Grandpa."

"They need to learn to speak American. Can't understand a word they say."

Shannon's heart sank. She took a deep breath. "Grandpa, I'm sure you don't mean that. You don't even know them."

"I don't need to know them. They're damn immigrants, just like their parents. They're all the same. Every damn one of 'em."

Shannon pursed her lips, then looked to the sky. It was time. "Mr. Walker —"

"Call me Grandpa, sweetie."

Shannon smiled sadly. "Grandpa, would you "read" my face and tell me what you see?"

"Shannon ..." Tony said, alarmed.

She silenced Tony with a look and Grandpa appeared confused.

"Read your face?"

"Yes. With your hands. I've heard that blind people can often "see" by touch."

He hesitated, then reached out. Shannon guided his hands to her face. He gently placed his palms on her cheeks, then traced his fingers along her features — her forehead, eyebrows, the bridge of her nose, her cheekbones, her lips.

"You're beautiful," he said softly. "Just like I knew you'd be."

Shannon lowered her head, took a deep breath, then looked back at him. "Grandpa, I'm Black."

He yanked his hand back and froze. A heavy silence fell, then he stared blankly.

"That's not possible," he said.

"Why? Because I don't speak how you think Black people speak? Because I like classic literature?"

"But you don't sound ... you don't act ..."

"Like what, Grandpa?" Shannon asked gently.

His hands fell away from her face. He leaned back on the bench, visibly shaken.

Tony moved beside him and rested his hand on his shoulder. "Grandpa, Shannon's mom is a literature professor at the university, and her dad's an architect."

"But ... but you're so ..." Grandpa struggled to find words.

"Normal? Yes. Just like those boys you heard, and Mr. Leibowitz, and Tony's Italian friend, Marco."

He sat in stunned silence until Shannon reached out and took his hand.

"You remember what Scout learns in *To Kill a Mockingbird?* 'Sometimes we're afraid of what we don't understand, but when we actually get to know others ... ' "s

"We see them for who they are," he finished quietly.

"Exactly."

He sat silently for a long moment. "I don't know what to say."

"You don't have to say anything. Sit here and enjoy your lunch."

They sat together in silence, Grandpa still holding Shannon's hand, his face a complex mixture of emotions. In that moment, she saw something break in him — not in a destructive way, but like a dam cracking to release waters long held back.

Over the following weeks, Shannon led Grandpa through a literary journey of diverse voices. They read *The Diary of a Young Girl* by Anne Frank, *Angela's Ashes* by Frank McCourt, and *They Came in Ships* by John E. McDonough. And with each story, she watched his world expand a little more.

One evening, as they sat on the porch, Mr. Leibowitz walked by with his dog. He hesitated, clearly used to avoiding the house.

"Evening, Leibowitz!" Grandpa called out. "Hot one today, isn't it?"

"Yes ... yes it is, Walker," Mr. Leibowitz said, surprised.

"Tony tells me that's a fine-looking dog you've got. What breed is he?"

Mr. Leibowitz approached cautiously. "She's a beagle mix. Her name is Bagel."

"Bagel the beagle," Grandpa said with a laugh. "That's a good one, Leibowitz."

Tony and Shannon exchanged amazed glances.

"You know, I had a dog when I could still see," Grandpa continued. "Australian Shepherd. Best friend I ever had."

"Would you like to pet Bagel? She's very gentle."

Grandpa reached his hand out. "I think I would."

As Mr. Leibowitz brought his dog closer, Shannon squeezed Grandpa's hand, pride swelling in her chest.

After Mr. Leibowitz left, Shannon moved her chair closer. "Grandpa, would you like to invite some people over one night? Maybe we could even start a book club."

He stopped rocking, then nodded. "I think I'd like that."

Two weeks later, the living room was filled with people of various ethnicities — Tony's friends and people from all walks of life. Shannon organized books while Grandpa sat in his armchair, looking more animated than she'd ever seen him.

Among the guests were Marco, David wearing his yarmulke, and the Chinese-American boys from the park with their parents.

"It was Shannon's idea to start this book club," Grandpa announced to the group, "and it looks like it's gotten off to a good start. But why stop here? If you know anyone who wants to come, bring 'em along. Everyone's welcome." He paused. "And we've got the best narrator in the world — our very own Shannon."

"I brought cannoli," Marco's mother said. "An old family recipe my parents brought from Napoli."

"Wonderful!" Grandpa replied genuinely. "I haven't had a good cannoli in years."

Marco leaned in and whispered jokingly, "That's a 'cannolo,' Grandpa. 'Cannoli' is plural."

Grandpa laughed. "I'll be sure to remember that, Marco, thanks."

Shannon slipped a new book into Grandpa's hands. "I brought something special today," she whispered.

"What's this?" he asked, feeling the braille on the cover.

"It's a Braille edition of To Kill a Mockingbird. I know you've resisted learning Braille, but I thought we could learn together."

His expression softened. He reached for her hand, paused to wipe a tear from his eye, then leaned over and kissed her cheek.

"Okay, everyone!" Tony announced. "Time to start our first official meeting of the Walker House Book Club!"

As everyone settled in, Grandpa patted his lap and pulled Shannon toward him.

"Thank you for helping an old blind man to finally see," he whispered.

Shannon kissed his cheek, her face radiant. "That's what friends are for."

Grandpa leaned back in his chair and smiled. Shannon knew that some kinds of blindness have nothing to do with eyes, and everything to do with the heart.

PART TWO

THE LOAN SHARK

In 1950s Brooklyn, fruit vendor Alphonse Marino struggles to provide for his family amidst poverty and prejudice. With no other choice, he resorts to the risky world of loan sharks when banks refuse to help.

As debts mount and loan sharks circle, Alphonse must balance hope, desperation, and integrity in a vibrant immigrant community filled with loyalty and hidden dangers.

With colorful streets, warm family ties, and a touch of supernatural intrigue, this story blends heart, humor, and suspense, asking what it means to survive — and who really holds the power.

TOUGH TIMES

Brooklyn, 1950

The neighborhood buzzed with life. Pushcarts lined the sidewalks, and women hung clothes to dry on ropes that were strung between tenement buildings. Children played stickball in the street, scattering when automobiles honked through. On one corner, children played in water spewing from an open fire hydrant.

Alphonse Marino, a squat man in his forties with a thick mustache, arranged fruit at his modest stand. He wore a stained apron and repeatedly wiped sweat from his brow. Despite the summer heat, his stand was vibrant with colorful produce, and crowded with customers.

He welcomed each customer with a smile, and proudly boasted of the day's deals. At the end of the day, he closed his stand and secured his fruit in a communal cold storage unit.

At the end of the day, I closed shop, trudged up the steps to my cramped two-bedroom apartment, lifted my head, and breathed deeply.

"I smell meatballs."

Maria Marino, my wife, with tired eyes and a warm smile, nodded as she served pasta to our children: Tony, a thin twelve-year-old with dark hair and an intelligent look; Rosa, a proud, determined nine-year-old; and Dante, a shy, reserved six-year-old, all seated at a small table.

When I took his seat, Maria brought me a large plate of pasta with two meatballs on the side, sprinkled with freshly grated cheese. I smiled and stared at Maria, my mouth agape.

"*Dove hai preso i bucatini?*" I asked. "Where did you get the bucatini?"

Maria's smile spread her chubby cheeks wide. "Concetta find in new shop in the Bronx. She goes once a week. She buy this for us." She paused, and pointed at me. "And speak English so kids learn."

I took a few bites, then looked at Maria. "Tell Concetta she getta free fruit."

Tony smiled. "That's 'gets' Papà, not 'getta.'"

My smile was beaming. I rubbed Tony's head. "At's-a my boy. You teach Papà good. I like."

~

Shouting was heard from the apartment next to us. The walls were thin, and if the neighbors argued, they were heard. And the neighbors always argued.

Maria walked over and banged on the wall. "*Basta*! I no want my kids to hear that trash."

Tony and his sister cleared the table and washed the dishes, then they sat back down and brought out the *scopa* cards. Tony shuffled them.

"Prepare to lose, Papà."

Maria walked over and kissed each of them on the cheek. When she got to Tony, she whispered to him, "*Sil gentile*, Antonio. Your brother and sister need to win too."

After the games were over, Maria took the kids to their bedroom and made sure they were tucked in, then she returned to the kitchen.

She brought a handful of papers and set them in front of me.

"So many?" I asked.

I went through the bills, my face growing more concerned with each one I set aside. Maria sat across from me, lines of worry etched on her face.

"How bad?"

I set my pencil down and covered my face with my hands. I didn't look up as Maria walked over. She put her hand on my shoulder.

"I know is bad, but the kids need shoes. I can patch mine, but ..."

I shook my head. "Maybe I get money and make bigger stand, then I sell more things — more than fruit." I felt the smile stretch my face. "I can sell peppers from Domenico. He grows great peppers. And —"

Maria smiled and rubbed the back of my neck, then rested her head on my shoulder. "I go to bed, Alphonse."

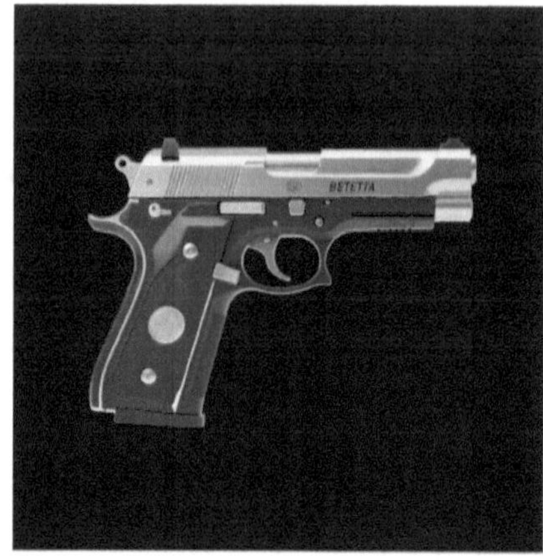

She walked to the bedroom but stood in the doorway and watched as Alphonse emptied his pockets and counted coins, then opened the small can they kept change in.

Maria held back tears, but after a moment she went to bed.

As she covered herself, she made the sign of the cross. "*Dio mio, abbiamo bisogno del tuo aiuto. Il mio Alphonse, lavora così duramente ed è un uomo buono. Ti prego, aiutaci.*" She prayed a long time, asking God to help her hardworking husband.

THE LOAN

The next day, I sat across from a loan officer at First National Bank. The officer, a pompous man in his fifties dressed in a suit, looked me over. His shoes were fancy, his tie was fancy, and he sat behind a large mahogany desk.

The loan officer lit a cigarette and flipped through the papers quickly before sliding them back. "I'm sorry, but we can't help you."

I scrunched up my eyes. "But —"

The loan officer stood and shook his head, then escorted me out of the bank.

I tried other banks but was rejected by them as well.

After leaving, I trudged down the busy sidewalk, moving aside to let people pass. I stopped at the building before the Bank of New York and looked into the mirrored glass, straightened my tie, brushed dirt from my clothes, then entered the bank, wearing a smile I didn't feel.

I was rejected at this bank so quickly, I barely had time to get comfortable in the plush chair they offered me.

I exited the bank, my head held low, and made my way to Brooklyn Savings and Loan, my hopes high. As I waited, I heard the manager whisper to the loan officer: "... immigrants."

I clenched my teeth and balled my fists, but I exited the bank and headed toward home.

Outside the window, a cab drove past. Inside it, Gianni, a boisterous man in his fifties with expressive hands, glanced up at the bank windows, his eyes briefly glowing.

As the day turned to dusk, I walked slowly, shoulders slumped. The street was narrow, lined with brownstones and iron balconies. As I neared the neighborhood, kids filled the street, yelling to each other in Italian as they played stickball.

Women gathered the laundry that had been drying in the fresh air all day and chatted with neighbors who did the same. At the corner, a man argued with a fishmonger, waving a scaly bass like it owed him money.

Up and down the street, women swept the stoops and sidewalks, cleaning off the dust that gathered throughout the day.

I broke into song as a nearby radio blared Sinatra music. I was almost home when I saw several friends sitting on a stoop across the street. They looked to be playing *scopa*.

I waved and yelled to them. "*Ciao, ragazzi! Tutto bene?*" (Hey, guys. All good?)

I passed a small Italian café where Gianni sat on a stoop drinking espresso and nibbling on a *sflogiatella* (pastry from Naples). He wore a comfortable, worn suit that somehow still looked stylish. A cigarette dangled from the left side of his lip.

"Ciao, Alphonse, *come va?*" Gianni asked.

I sighed. "Not so good."

Gianni patted the stoop beside him, and I sat down heavily, the weight of the day causing me to land hard.

"So, no luck at the bank?" Gianni asked.

I laughed sarcastically. "You mean banks." I held up three fingers. "Three turned me down."

Gianni sipped his espresso. "Maybe you talk to Renzo."

"Not so desperate — yet," I said.

"Ah! But you think about it, eh?"

"What's the point in dreaming if it costs more than my business?"

"But the money — it be nice, no?"

"*Si, Gianni. Sarebbe bello*," (Yes, the money would be nice.)

"So?"

"I don't know," I said. "How much vig Renzo charge?"

Gianni laughed, slapping his knee. "For a paisan, he make special deal — five percent vig."

I shook his head. "Still a lot."

"Not so much. You borrow $1,000, you pay $50 vig each week."

"And if I can't pay?" I asked, followed by a sarcastic chuckle.

"You know what happens. Remember Paulo from The Avenue?"

"I visit him in the hospital," I said.

"But Renzo take care of his familia while he sick," Gianni pointed out. "And the banks? They maybe don't break legs, but they trick you."

Gianni leaned in conspiratorially and whispered, "They say you have five years to pay the loan, and only charge 9%. But miss a payment and Signor *Banchiere* pay a visit." He paused. "He embarrass you in front of your neighbors and family and then — he raise your interest. Now, 9% is 24%, and then — *Sei fregato*." (You're in trouble).

"And what about Renzo?"

Gianni shrugged. "Renzo is fair. He charge you a little more — maybe twenty-five percent, maybe more. And he also adds vig."

Gianni pointed his fat finger at me. "You get maybe a month to pay back — if he likes you — but then you gotta pay. If you no pay, he come lookin' for you, just like the banks."

After a pause, he continued, "But when Renzo come, he no embarrass you. He tell your family and neighbors he come for something else. If you no have cash," Renzo whispers "He see you the next day, and trust me — he will. When you turn a corner there he is."

The streetlights flickered on, and a police car slowly drove by, watching everything on both sides of the street. Gianni waved but cursed them under his breath. "La *polizia* — only for the rich."

"Where I find Renzo?" I asked.

"You ask for his help now?" Gianni smiled.

"Just asking."

"Don't worry. Renzo finds you. But if you want, I mention something to him. See what he says."

ANOTHER SOURCE

That night, Gianni strolled down lower Montague Street in Brooklyn Heights, listening to the boisterous shouts of kids playing games, their voices a mixture of Italian, Irish, Yiddish, and more.

Steam rose from a manhole, and across the street, a fruit vendor touted the end-of-the-day specials in a sing-song fashion.

Gianni deftly avoided a crack in the sidewalk where it had been raised up by nearby tree roots. Then he took in the smells of simmering sauce, roasted peppers, and garlic.

As he moved up the street, it grew quieter, and the storefronts were replaced by brownstones with manicured gardens, and surrounded by iron fences and gates.

Gianni slowed his pace as he admired the splendor of the old houses, many built more than one hundred years ago. *Not bad for a city built on bones.*

He took one last gulp of his espresso, tossed it into a trash bin, then continued his walk. When he reached Renzo's house, he knocked on the door and waited.

Renzo, a muscular man in his forties, with scars on his knuckles, opened the door and laughed, embracing Gianni and hugging him tightly. "What do you want, old man?"

Gianni laughed, brushed by Renzo, and took a seat on a lush sofa sitting against the wall. "It's neck and neck who is older, my friend. Neither one of us is a bambino anymore."

Gianni paused. "And maybe you are growing rusty. You didn't sense me coming."

"Gianni, I know you for what ... two, maybe three hundred years. Should I worry?"

Gianni brushed his hand in the air, walked over, and picked a book from Renzo's bookshelf. "Dante. Always so dramatic." After a pause, he asked, "How many times you read this?"

"Not so many."

Gianni sat, suddenly looking ancient despite his appearance. "Alphonse needs money."

"Honest man. Good soul. Rare in this age. More rare in Brooklyn."

"You give him time if he need it?"

"*Sempre. Soprattutto con i tuoi preferiti,*" Renzo said. (I always do, especially with your favorites.)

"You no give time to Arturo?"

Renzo scowled. "He gamble the money and lose it."

Renzo leaned back and smiled. "But I take care of his family while he recover."

"That is why we been working together for ... how long now?"

"I stop counting after so long."

Renzo laughed and poured two glasses of red wine. He sat and took a sip. Gianni toasted him and sipped his as well.

"Tastes like Old Country," Gianni said.

"It *is* Old Country."

They clinked glasses again, both briefly showing a mysterious glow of light in their eyes.

"*Cent'anni*," Gianni toasted, wishing Renzo to live a hundred years. "The scales must always balance."

Renzo leaned back, eyes wide open. "Only one hundred?"

Gianni laughed. "Then we toast what?"

Renzo clinked glasses with Gianni again. "*Justitia et misericordia.*" (Justice and mercy.)

"When you start speaking Latin?" Gianni asked.

"I grow tired of the way we speak."

Gianni finished his wine and got up to leave. "Go see Alphonse. He maybe ready." After a pause, he added, "And maybe you go see those *banchieri?*"

Renzo pressed his lips together and shook his head. "*Mio caro amico, sai che non posso farlo.*" (My dear friend, you know I can't do that.)

Gianni shrugged and then broke into laughter. "You have reputation as tough guy, but you have soft heart." He paused. "*Così sia. Forse lo farò.*" (So be it. Maybe I'll do it.)

Meanwhile, at the Marino apartment, Maria sat at the table mending shoes. The heels were worn through, and the leather cracked. She winced as she pricked her finger and blood dropped onto her dress.

"*Che sfortuna.*" She muttered in Italian, lamenting her bad luck.

Tony entered, schoolbooks under his arm and hiding his shirt. He ran toward the bedroom, his head hung low.

Maria looked up and raised her voice. "*Torna qui*, Antonio." (Come here.)

Tony turned and stood before his mother. "What?"

Maria took his books. There was a tear in his shirt. "What happened?"

"The kids at school," Tony reluctantly explained. "They called us dagos and wops. And they said we smelled like garlic."

Maria's face hardened. She pulled Tony close. "You are Marino. Those boys, their families were immigrants too, once."

"But papà's only got a fruit stand. Jimmy's father owns a factory. And they have a car."

"Money no make a man."

Tony nodded, unconvinced.

"Things get better soon," Maria said. "Your papà works hard."

The younger children burst in, playing. Maria looked at the holes in the kids' shoes, the torn clothes, then at the nearly empty pantry. Her determination wavered for just a moment.

The next day at the fruit stand, Alphonse arranged peaches while keeping an eye on a tough-looking man leaning against a lamp post.

~

Renzo smoked a cigarette, watching Alphonse from across the street. After a long drag, he tossed the smoke to the sidewalk and crushed it out.

Renzo watched as Maria brought Alphonse lunch. He chose that moment to cross over.

"Bella frutta," he said in a rough voice.

~

Alphonse tensed as Maria stood beside him.

"Can I help, signore?" Maria asked.

"Just lookin' what you got, signora," Renzo said. "*Tuo marito ha un buon occhio per la qualità.*" (Your husband have good eye for quality.)

"Grazie," Maria said with a smile. "He works hard."

Maria returned to other customers, and Renzo leaned in to speak to me. "Gianni say you need money."

"Maybe a little," I said nervously.

"Talk to me tonight — at Angelo's."

I nodded, but continued to cast glances at Renzo as he walked down the street.

As customers came to his stand, I asked the ones who knew best about Renzo.

"Hey, Sal, you know anything about Renzo?" I asked.

"Who?"

"You know — the paisan who lends money?"

Sal looked all around, then shook his head. "*Uno con cui è meglio non avere a che fare,*" he said, saying Renzo is someone who is better not to deal with.

I talked to several other customers but got similar answers.

"I know Renzo," one customer said. "He show up when you need money — or if you no pay."

"Renzo? The best," another told me. "He lend my brother money, and now he do good with his restaurant."

After shutting down the fruit stand, I told Maria I had to see another person about a loan.

She closed her eyes and sobbed. "Not worth it. It only make you feel bad. Just stay home."

I shook my head. "No take long. *Promesso*."

AN ALTERNATIVE

That night, I joined Renzo in the back room of Angelo's Trattoria. Renzo sat at a table, a bottle of grappa in front of him.

Angelo brought two espressos, and after he set them on the table, Renzo poured a little grappa into each. He then wrote numbers onto a napkin.

"You need five hundred, you pay back six hundred in four weeks," Renzo said.

"That's twenty percent!"

Renzo shrugged. "You good witt numbers, Alphonse. Five percent a week. Not so much when you think that way." After a pause, he continued, "But I no bank. You want bank money, go ahead. They give you nothing. My money is same as theirs."

I hesitated, then extended my hand. "Are there papers to sign?"

Renzo laughed and hit the table with the palm of his hand. "You make me laugh, Alphonse. I like you. Your word is all I need."

Renzo poured more grappa, then raised his glass in a toast. "Cent'anni!"

One week later, I helped a driver unload a truck filled with fruit, then arranged them on my stand. Using Renzo's money, I expanded my stand and bought more produce. Business picked up, with more customers coming each day.

I counted more money at the end of the day, while Maria sewed new clothes for the kids. She looked happier, singing and humming all day.

Before the day began, I ran to see Gianni, who was sitting on the stoop, smoking a cigarette.

I leaned down and kissed Gianni on the cheek. "You a saint. Renzo give me the money and now my business grows."

Gianni smiled. "Just make a sure you pay Renzo back, or else ..." He imitated a man swinging a bat.

"No worries. And Grazie. *Grazie mille*," I said. "Now I gotta open the stand."

Three Weeks Later

I now had a bigger stand, more inventory, and even an employee, who was busy helping customers when Renzo walked up.

"Four weeks, today."

"I know," I said, prepared. I handed an envelope to Renzo, who counted it and nodded.

"*Sempre un piacere fare affari*," Renzo said, indicating it was always a pleasure doing business.

"Actually ..." I hesitated. "I might need a bit more. This do so good, I maybe open one more — down by St. Maria's."

Renzo looked me over with eyes that saw everything. "Maybe you see the bank first. You have good business to show now."

"I no think they help."

"If they no help — then, come see me."

Renzo walked away and called back over his shoulder, "*Speriamo che non ci vediamo più*." (I hope I don't see you again.)

The next day, I visited Brooklyn Savings and Loan. The same loan officer who had rejected me before was closing up for the day, but I convinced the man to let me in.

"I was here two months ago," I said.

The loan officer sneered. "Nothing has changed."

"But it has!" I said. "I got lots more business and more fruit."

The loan officer peered over the rims of his glasses, stepped close to me, and whispered, "All I see is an immigrant dressed in a cheap, dirty suit."

I got up and left, a downtrodden look on my face.

Later that day, Gianni sat on the same stoop, smoking a cigarette when I walked by, head hung low.

"Ciao, Alphonse. *Come va?*" Gianni greeted me.

"Not so good. I maybe need help from Renzo again," Alphonse said.

Gianni nodded. "I take care of it."

THE PAYBACK

That night, the loan officer exited the Brooklyn Savings and Loan, waving to the security guard, who whistled to a cabbie sitting nearby.

The cabbie, who was actually Gianni with his features slightly altered, pulled to the curb. "Need a ride, signore?"

The loan officer sat in the back of the cab, checking his watch. He handed Gianni a slip of paper with an address written on it. "Take Fifth Avenue north. It's faster."

The cabbie looked in the rearview and smiled. "I no think so,

Signor Banker. I pick up two others not so long ago, and I find a faster way."

The cab suddenly accelerated, turning down a side street toward the waterfront.

"What are you doing? Stop the damn car. Stop it!" The loan officer panicked as the car sped through the narrow streets.

Gianni drove faster, smiling all the while. He dodged dumpsters and piles of trash lying on the sides, and just before reaching the pier, he jumped out, rolling onto the street.

The car raced across a cross street and crashed through a railing and into the dark water below, quickly sinking.

Gianni watched from the shadows as bubbles rose to the surface. He brushed the dirt from his coat, and as he walked off, a soft shimmer passed over him — faint but unnatural. His features shifted, changing back to his normal appearance, then he straightened his jacket and walked away, whistling a merry tune.

The next night, Gianni walked leisurely down the street, a cigarette dangling from his mouth.

Renzo sat at a table outside a small café. When he saw Gianni, he called out to him. "Gianni, *aspetta per me*." (Wait for me.)

Renzo crossed the street and moved alongside Gianni. He looked all around before speaking. "You do that to banchieri?"

"It had to be done."

Renzo set his lips firmly. "I would do different."

"*Lo so, amico mio. È per questo che lavoriamo così bene come squadra*," Gianni said. (I know, my friend. That's why we work so well as a team.)

Renzo shrugged and clapped Gianni on the back. "*A domani*, Gianni." (See you tomorrow).

Gianni continued his walk until he saw Alphonse sitting on the stoop outside his building. He sat next to him, and Alphonse offered him a sip of wine from a bottle he held.

"Good vino, Alphonse," Gianni said.

"You hear what happened to that banker from Brooklyn Savings?" Alphonse asked.

"Bad accident," Gianni replied innocently. "His car dive right in the river."

"That make three bankers in three weeks," Alphonse noted suspiciously.

"*Non c'è due senza tre,*" Gianni shrugged. (All bad things happen in threes.)

"Who are you my friend — *veramente?* (really)" Alphonse asked, studying Gianni.

"Just a friend who believes good people deserve good fortune."

Gianni's eyes briefly glowed with an otherworldly light, but when Alphonse blinked, Gianni appeared as a normal old Italian man again.

"*Alcuni debiti vanno saldati. Alcune giustizie vanno servite,*" Gianni said. (Some debts need paying. Some justice needs serving.)

"And Renzo?" Alphonse asked.

"He works for me, in a way." Gianni smiled.

They clinked glasses and looked up to admire the Brooklyn skyline, lit up against the night. It was a beacon of light, and a beacon of hope.

PART THREE

A PERFECT MURDER?

A Perfect Murder is a gripping whodunit where secrets and betrayals unravel in a quiet Texas suburb. Alyssa Ellis is brutally murdered, and suspicion falls on family and friends as detectives race against time to piece together the clues.

Tensions flare at a poker night filled with hidden motives and desperate lies, leading investigators through twists of loyalty, deceit, and shattered relationships. In a story built on red herrings and shifting alibis, everyone is a suspect and no one's innocence is assured.

This suspenseful drama is a puzzle that asks — how far will someone go to protect what's theirs?

MURDER FOR MONEY

Alyssa Ellis walked into the living room with a crossword puzzle in hand. She was in her forties, perky and intelligent, looking forward to a quiet evening. Just as she was about to sit down, a ringing sound came from the guest room.

"Tom, is that you?"

She set the puzzle aside and walked to the guest room. Her hand turned the knob and reached for the light switch. A person stepped toward her in the darkness. She gasped and stepped back.

As the figure came into focus, Alyssa relaxed. "What in God's name are you sneaking around for? You scared me."

The person stepped forward and swung a tire iron at her head. She fell to the floor. Blood pooled underneath her as the person stepped away from the body and went up the steps.

Alyssa crawled toward the phone lying on the floor. Her eyes were covered with blood and her vision blurred, but she made it to the phone and dialed 9-1-1, blood smearing on the keypad.

"Help. Need help."

The person returned and hit her two more times on the head.

. . .

Detectives Carl Hitchens and Dave Abbott pulled to the curb outside the Ellis house. Hitchens was in his forties, slim, somber and focused. Abbott was forty, tall, intense, all business.

The front door was locked, but Hitchens found the back door open. They went inside.

A woman's body lay on the floor with blood pooled underneath her. Hitchens knelt and checked for a pulse.

"No vitals. But she's still warm."

Abbott scrolled through the phone.

"Husband's number is first on her favorites list. Tom Ellis. And in the notes section, it says poker on Thursday nights at Ed's."

"I guess we need to see Ed."

Tom set the table while Alyssa finished cooking. She made her famous roast, and the house was ripe with a rich and savory aroma, complemented by the tantalizing smell of onions and mushrooms.

As Tom sat down, Alyssa popped the cork on one of their favorite wines, a Brunello they had found on a vacation in Italy. She brought the meat to the table while Tom poured two glasses. He then took a deep breath, and sighed.

"Just the smell of that makes me so damn hungry."

Alyssa put a few slices on her plate, then turned to Tom. "I hope you enjoy the aroma because the roast is for me. You can eat at the game."

Tom clenched his jaw. "What the hell does that mean?"

She sipped her wine and stared. "I met with the accountant today, and he asked me about several unexplained withdrawals."

Tom knew he was in trouble. "Sorry," he said, feeling his throat tighten.

"Sorry doesn't cut it. Straighten up, or you'll be on your own. I don't work my ass off so you can lose the money gambling."

Tom reached for her hand, but she yanked it back. "You can't sweet-talk me this time."

"I wasn't trying to. I just —"

"If you want to play cards, go! But if you lose, you better find a way to pay for it on your own."

Tom tried to sound confident. "Don't worry. I'll win tonight."

THE POKER GAME

Ed Richards greeted Tom at his door and showed him to the kitchen. An octagonal table sat in the eating area with eight chairs surrounding it, but only four had chips. Ed gestured to Owen and R.V. Skelton, who were already seated.

"Where the hell is everybody?" Tom asked.

"Just you, me, Owen, and R.V.," Ed said. "We can play four-handed and hope others show, or we can play pinochle. But either way, y'all better be hungry because Mary bought a HoneyBaked ham and three dozen rolls. And Shawna made her special sauce."

Tom pushed his chair back and looked at the clock as he headed to the island.

Owen swigged his drink and wiped his mouth with a napkin. "I hope Mary got different rolls; last time they were too fresh."

R.V. squeezed past Owen's chair on his way to get coffee. "Shit, if all I had to worry about was fresh rolls, I'd be pissin' with the big dogs; besides, all I had for dinner were a couple of hot dogs. Being laid off sucks."

Owen patted his belly and laughed. "I'm not one to talk, R.V., but from the looks of it, you ain't missed many meals in your life."

"Of course, I ain't, dumb shit. You're not supposed to miss meals."

Ed counted the chips and put $500 at each seat. "Cough up your buy-ins. The game is Texas Hold 'em: Pot limit, with $5 and $10 blinds."

Owen handed the deck to Tom, then tossed five dollars in. Tom dealt the cards, picked up his two, and squeezed them open. Owen bet fifty causing Tom to smile. He stayed quiet until it was time for him to act. "Raise a hundred."

Owen tossed his cards face down and cursed.

Later, the doorbell rang, and Ed started to get up, but the sound of footsteps bounding down the stairs along with Shawna's voice stopped him.

"I got it, Dad."

In the foyer, she answered the door, and Tom's son Ron stepped inside. They moved to the corner, and he kissed her passionately.

"God, I missed you. It's been weeks!" Shawna said.

"Weeks isn't long." Ron laughed. "I'll probably be gone that long on business trips; besides, I'll figure out a way to get you into a school near me, then we can get a house."

Shawna grabbed both of his hands with hers. "Did you come by to see me, or to talk to your mom about helping us with the house?"

"Mom thinks we'll squander the money, but I'll figure it out."

"My dad's the same way. He says all I know how to do is shop, but when we're married, we'll show them."

Ron pulled her closer and kissed her again. "It won't be long. Count on it."

Shawna hugged him tightly and offered a smile. "I'm not worried. You can't resist my charms."

"You've got that right, but hey, gotta go, babe," Ron said.

Ron rushed into the kitchen and hugged Tom. "Sorry for the rush, Dad. I've gotta prepare for a meeting. We're working on a big deal. But don't worry, I'll stop by on my way home."

"You better," Tom said, then he shuffled the deck, yawned, and stretched.

"Late night?" Owen asked.

Tom nodded. "Damn near all night. We had a wellhead blow. We lost a shitload of oil, *and* a few men got hurt bad enough to be hospitalized."

"How much oil?"

"About 50,000 barrels before we capped it."

R.V.'s phone rang, and he stepped onto the patio to talk.

~

"Hey, darlin'. What's up?" R.V. said.

"Ritchie got arrested for drugs."

"Shit! Where is he?"

"The cops are holding him; they said he's going to rehab or jail."

"Then let's get him in rehab."

"That'll cost ten thousand dollars," his wife said, her voice defeated.

R.V. walked in circles while talking. "I'll think of something. I'm not letting him go to jail."

R.V. tapped on the window and yelled to Tom. "Before you deal, join me on the porch."

Tom walked out with R.V., who looked at the guys in the kitchen before speaking.

"I need that money you owe me," he said. "I was laid off, and my boy's in trouble. I'm in dire straits."

"I heard you say that earlier. When did you get laid off?"

R.V. paced the deck and jiggled the change in his pocket. He stared at Tom and shook his head. "Christ, it's been two months. Didn't Alyssa tell you?"

"Why would she know anything?"

"Because it was her goddamn consulting firm that made the recommendations. Now I'm screwed. I'm two months late on my mortgage, and they're threatening foreclosure next month. I can't pay my kid's tuition, and to top it off, the son of a bitch got arrested tonight. I'm gonna need ten grand to keep him out of jail."

Tom looked everywhere but at R.V. "Shit, I'm sorry. I didn't know."

"I hear you, but sorry doesn't pay my mortgage. Tell that to Alyssa."

"Don't worry. I'll get your money."

"You said that before, Tom, but I need it now."

"If I had it, I'd pay you back. But I can't get it from Alyssa."

They stepped into the kitchen just as Shawna entered.

"Any of y'all need anything while I'm here? Want a sandwich, Owen?" she asked.

"Thanks, but don't trouble yourself," Owen said.

"It's no trouble. It'll only take me a minute."

"It's all right. I'll get it later."

Ed laughed. "Don't take offense. Owen's not worried about causing you trouble; he's worried you might have germs on your hands."

Shawna laughed as she walked out of the kitchen and headed up the stairs.

"Kids that age scare me. When mine was that young, I used to keep track of everywhere he went," R.V. said.

"I've got it covered, R.V. Got one of those GPS tracking apps that tells me where she is, and where she's been."

"My kid would've been pissed if I did that to him."

"Shawna's only twenty. I told her about this when I got it, but it's been a while. She probably forgot."

Tom yawned twice in a row. "Ed, I'm gonna take a quick nap. Wake me in forty minutes. You'll have to play pinochle until I get up."

R.V. checked his pocket and came up empty. "Shit, I'm out of chaw. Guess I need to run and get some. Can't play cards without it."

Ed grimaced. "That's a nasty habit, R.V."

R.V. grabbed a coat from the closet and headed out the door. "I'll be back shortly."

Forty minutes later, Tom walked in from the bedroom and took his seat. He riffled his chips and smiled while Ed shuffled the cards.

"I'm back, and rested. And ready to win."

Tom squeezed his cards and looked at a pair of tens. "Bet fifty."

Everyone folded but R.V.

The dealer turned over three cards, a seven, five, and ten. Tom stared at his pair of tens and bet one hundred. R.V. folded, and Tom raked in the pot.

THE DETECTIVES ARRIVE

Ed was shuffling the deck when flashing lights appeared outside. Then the doorbell rang.

"Damn, what the hell is it now?" Ed said.

He opened the front door to see two men in suits wearing stoic expressions. The taller one reached out his hand.

"I'm Detective Carl Hitchens, and this is Detective Dave Abbott."

Ed took a step back to block their view of the kitchen. "Detectives, how can I help you?"

Abbott grinned. "We're not here about the game, sir. We'd like to speak with Mr. Ellis."

R.V. leaned over and looked toward the front door, then he whispered to Tom and Owen. "Cops."

Tom slouched in his seat. "Just when I was winning."

Ed opened the door wider, stepped aside, and smiled. "Come on in. Tom's at the table."

Ed led the detectives into the kitchen. He gestured to Tom and nodded to the detectives.

"Mr. Ellis, would you step outside with us for a moment?" Abbott asked.

Tom looked quizzically at him, then set his cards face-down. "I'll only be a minute."

Tom went outside with the detectives. Hitchens lit a smoke.

"What's this about?" Tom asked.

"Sir, someone broke into your house and attacked your wife," Abbott said.

Tom grabbed Hitchens' shoulders, then ran for his car, but Hitchens stopped him.

"We can't go there right now, sir. CSU is processing the scene."

"Processing the scene? Is Alyssa —"

Hitchens placed his arm on Tom's shoulder. "I'm sorry to say, Mr. Ellis, but your wife is gone."

Tom staggered back and grabbed hold of the detective's arm. He buried his head in his hands and cried. "It can't! How could it happen?"

Dave Abbott turned to Tom and spoke softly. "Mr. Ellis, she was brutally attacked. Do you know —?"

Tom shook his head. "Hell no! Why would anyone hurt her?"

Tom punched the brick wall, drawing blood on his knuckles. "Goddamn!"

Hitchens took hold of Tom's arm, then led him inside. "Dave, how about you go back to the scene? I'll stay with Mr. Ellis."

Hitchens led Tom to the living room, wrapped up his hand, and then sat next to him on the sofa.

"Mr. Ellis, let's go to the kitchen. I need to speak with the others," he said.

Tom pulled out his phone and called Ron. "Ron, it's Dad. I've got bad news."

"Something happen?" Ron asked.

"There was a break-in at the house."

Tom held the phone away from his mouth. His hands trembled and his voice choked up. "Oh Christ, Ron. Somebody killed your mom. She's dead."

"Oh my God. Oh my God! I'm coming right up, Dad."

"I'm at Ed's house."

Hitchens was leaning against the kitchen wall when Abbott entered. Tom sat in the back, his head buried in his hands.

WE HAVE A FEW QUESTIONS

Hitchens stood before the table and spoke to all of them. "In case you didn't hear, Mrs. Ellis was murdered tonight, and we have to ask a few questions," Hitchens said to all the players. "We'll start in the living room but may have to take it to the station."

Ed put his arms around Tom and patted his back.

"I didn't even get to patch things up," Tom said to Ed. "We argued, and I left angry."

"Don't worry, Tom," Ed said, then whispered. "And don't say anything. Wait for your lawyer."

Hitchens pointed to Owen and crooked his finger. "You first."

Owen walked into the living room, shaking his head. "Can't goddamn believe it. She wasn't a saint, but damn, she didn't deserve this."

The living room had a fireplace, a sofa, and two stiff-backed chairs. The light from two lamps reflected off the tables.

Hitchens sat on the sofa, facing the fireplace, and Owen sat in a chair. He leaned close and whispered. "What happened?"

"We can't discuss the case, but do you know anyone who wished her harm?" Hitchens asked.

"No one I can think of, but she ran a tight ship — at work and home."

"Tough, huh?"

"Don't get me wrong; she didn't deserve this, but she kept Tom on a tight leash — a damn tight leash."

"How about work?"

"I don't know a lot of people she worked with, but one time we were bidding on the same job and she wormed her way into the winning bid. And not quite legally."

Hitchens cast a sideways glance at Owen. "I'd say that gives you motive."

"It's money, Detective. Not something you'd kill for."

Hitchens jotted down notes. "Has everyone been here all night?"

Owen paused. "I think ... yeah."

Owen sat up and snapped his fingers. "No, wait. R.V. ran to get some dip, but he was only gone a few minutes."

"But Mr. Ellis was here?"

"Yeah, Tom took a short nap; otherwise, he was in the kitchen."

Hitchens jotted down a few more notes. "Okay, that's all for now. Would you ask R.V. to come in?"

Hitchens leaned back on the sofa. "When I asked Owen if everyone had been here all night, he hesitated."

"Christ's sake, maybe he just hesitated," R.V. replied. "Nobody went anywhere but me. I ran to get dip."

"So nobody was gone for more than a minute or two?"

R.V. paused. "Tom took a quick nap, but he wasn't more than twenty or thirty minutes, and I doubt I was more than fifteen. Maybe twenty."

Hitchens looked at R.V. quizzically. "Owen said Tom was on a tight leash?"

R.V. laughed sarcastically. "He's being nice. Alyssa has all the money, and she controls it. There's not much Tom can do without her OK."

"Did he have reason to harm her?"

R.V. brushed his hand in the air. "Oh, hell no! Tom wouldn't hurt a soul; besides, he worshipped her."

"And he never left the house?"

R.V. shook his head. "I wasn't here the whole time he napped, but the others would have seen him if he left."

"Where's the bedroom?"

R.V. pointed to a door about ten feet away, then got up and led Hitchens to it.

Hitchens entered the bedroom and then walked into the bathroom. It had two vanities, a shower, and a Jacuzzi. At the end of the bathroom was a door.

Hitchens opened the door and he and R.V. stepped onto a small porch with a few steps leading to the yard. A large weeping willow sat on the left, inside a six-foot picket fence.

Hitchens pointed to a house across the bayou. "Isn't that the Ellis house?"

R.V. looked over and nodded. "It is, but I told you earlier; there's no way Tom did this."

"We never know what a person is, or isn't, capable of."

"One more thing. How do we know you didn't stop by the Ellis house when you went to get dip?" Hitchens asked.

"Because, scumbag, you can ask the clerk at the bodega."

R.V. took his seat, and Hitchens looked around the table and pointed to Tom.

"Mr. Ellis, would you come with me?" he asked.

Tom took a seat in a stiff-backed chair by the fireplace.

"What do you need?" Tom asked.

Hitchens held his notepad in front of him. "A few of the men said you were gone for half an hour or more."

"I was tired, so I napped. Now I wish I'd just gone home."

"Did you leave the house?"

Tom looked at him as if he were nuts. "You fuckin' prick. Are you asking me if I killed Alyssa?"

"My apologies, sir, but somebody did, and we have to eliminate every possible suspect."

Ed opened the front door just as Ron dried his eyes. Ed hugged him and patted his back.

"I'm so sorry, Ron. I can't believe it. Your mom was a special woman," Ed said.

"I need to see Dad."

Tom raced into the foyer, followed by Hitchens. Tom wrapped his arms around Ron and both of them cried. They were still hugging when Abbott pulled Ron aside.

"Would you mind coming into the living room with me?" Abbott asked.

Ron sat on the couch and rested his arm on the side.

"Are you up for a few questions? I understand if you're not," Abbott said.

Ron nodded, then Abbott pulled out his notepad. "We found a few blades of wet grass on the floor next to your mom. Any idea—?"

"Then whoever killed her, came in the back door," Ron said.

"Why do you say that?"

"The back sprinklers go on at seven, but the front ones don't go on until midnight. And Mom didn't usually lock the back door."

Detective Hitchens stepped into the kitchen and gestured to Ed. "I'm going to check on a few things outside the bathroom door, so if you see anyone there, it's me."

"Call me if you need anything," Ed replied.

"Do we have your permission to search the house?"

"Of course. No problem."

Hitchens walked to the outside door, flipped the light switch on, then opened it.

Hitchens walked onto the porch and inspected the railings and stairs but saw no signs of recent usage. He then walked underneath the large weeping willow tree inside the corner of the fence. It was a big tree with thick branches.

He looked up and saw a window above, one with easy access to the tree limbs.

Hitchens called Ron and Tom to the living room. He stood when they entered, and gestured for them to sit in the chairs.

"I don't want to upset either of you, but we need a suspect. Most murders are committed by people the victim knows, so if it's not either of you, who's left? Who do you know that meant her harm or who would benefit from her death?" Hitchens asked.

Hitchens looked to Tom, but Tom's head was buried in his hands. Ron patted Tom's back and turned to Hitchens.

"My mom has money, but only Dad and I are in her will, and she promised to give Shawna and I money for a house," Ron said.

"So it's just coincidence that you're in town and your mother is killed when you stand to inherit a lot of money?" Hitchens asked.

Ron gritted his teeth and balled his hands into fists. "You can shove coincidence up your ass sideways, Detective. Stop trying to find an easy suspect and do some real investigating."

Tom nodded. He looked as if he would say something, but then just nodded again. Hitchens ignored Ron and turned to Tom.

"What about you, Mr. Ellis? What are your thoughts on the matter?"

"I've got nothing. Alyssa and I had arguments over the years, but nothing that mattered," Tom replied, then paused. "One thing — Never mind."

"What were you going to say?"

"It's just that ..."

Tom leaned forward and whispered. "I owe R.V. a good deal of money, and he asked about it tonight."

"How much do you owe him?"

"It's a sizable chunk — $20,000."

Abbott entered the room, and Hitchens stood and greeted him. Abbott whispered something, and Hitchens whispered back.

"Mr. Ellis, how about you and Ron stay here while I go with Dave?" Hitchens said.

Hitchens and Abbott conferred in the foyer, keeping their voices low. Hitchens walked toward the kitchen and called Ed.

"Mr. Richards, I've talked to almost everyone. The only ones left are your wife and daughter. Can you ask them to join us in the living room, please? And one at a time," he said.

Hitchens walked into the living room and told Ron and Tom they could leave. As they exited the room, Mary and Shawna came down the stairs.

Shawna stopped and hugged Ron as they passed in the hall, and Mary continued to the living room.

"I'm sorry, Ron. Your mom was sweet. I still can't believe it," Shawna said.

Mary sat with her hands folded on her lap.

"Detective, how may I help?" she asked.

"Ma'am, do you know any reason why anyone would harm Mrs. Ellis?" Hitchens asked.

Mary shook her head vehemently. "I've heard Alyssa could be a tough boss, but all I've ever seen is her kindness, and I know everyone at the tennis club feels the same way."

"I've heard she kept Mr. Ellis on a tight leash."

"And he needed to be, but it wasn't tight enough to choke him."

"Did they have infidelity problems?"

Mary laughed. "Heavens, no. They loved each other, and as far as I know, Tom's gambling was their only problem."

"Okay, Mrs. Richards, thank you."

As Mary stood, Hitchens called Shawna. "Shawna, would you mind taking a seat? I have a few questions."

Shawna kissed Ron on the cheek and then took a seat on the cushion next to Hitchens.

Hitchens smiled, then shifted to face Shawna. "I was chatting with my Dave about how the willow tree must have been great when you were growing up. You know, like when teenagers want to sneak out."

Shawna snorted. "Are you kidding me? My dad probably had sensors on the limbs."

"So he was a stickler for the rules?"

"Still is. I need to tell him where I am at all times and call if I'm going to be somewhere else."

"Can't say that I blame him. I'm almost as bad with my son. If I had a daughter, I'd do the same."

Shawna turned her head to the side. "I don't like it, but I understand."

"Have you been home all night?" Hitchens asked.

Shawna sat up straight and folded her hands on her lap. "I fixed food for the game, then I went upstairs. After that, I fell asleep until you came."

"And you didn't go out?"

Shawna shook her head.

"What were you doing between 8:30 and 9:00?"

"I guess I was sleeping."

Abbott looked at his notepad. "Ron called at 8:45. Did you call him back to see what he wanted?"

Shawna searched her pocket. "I don't know where my phone is. Maybe I left it in my room."

She got up to leave, but Hitchens stopped her. "We can check later; besides, we're about done for now. Would you mind asking your dad to come in?"

Ed walked in and sat down across from Hitchens.

"Shawna said you wanted to talk," Ed said.

"We do, Mr. Richards, but you're not going to like what we say."

"What the hell does that mean?"

"We have reason to believe Shawna had something to do with Mrs. Ellis's murder. There are other suspects, but none with motive and opportunity as strong as Shawna's."

Ed laughed. "Detective, if you knew Shawna, you'd know how ridiculous that is; She's engaged to Alyssa's son."

"Being engaged isn't an alibi, and we already know that she didn't answer a call from Ron at 8:45, the time of the murder, and —"

Ed scoffed and brushed his hand in the air. "She's a suspect because she didn't answer a call? That's bullshit, and I can prove it."

Ed pulled out his cell phone and navigated to the app used for tracking by GPS. He typed in Shawna's name and waited.

"This is a tracking app that shows where her phone is in real-time. It also shows where she's been," Ed explained. "I just requested her tracking information for the night."

"How accurate is it?" Hitchens asked.

"Down to about 50 or 60 feet."

Within seconds, the app pulled up a map showing her at Ed's location. But the history of where she'd been showed her at Tom's house at 8:45, the approximate time of the murder.

"Explain that," Hitchens said.

Ed shook his head and furrowed his brow. His cheeks turned red as if he was embarrassed. "Let me reboot the app."

Ed quit the app, restarted the phone, and opened the app again. After entering her name, the same stats appeared.

"That can't be. It can't! Shawna would never do anything to Alyssa. We'll get this straightened out," Ed insisted.

Ed stepped into the hallway and called Shawna. "Shawna! Get down here."

Shawna sat and smiled. Ed sat across from her, trembling.

"What the hell were you doing at Ron's house tonight?" Ed demanded.

Shawna shook her head. "I wasn't at Ron's house."

"Don't lie to me, girl. I have you on a GPS tracking app, and it shows you there when Alyssa was killed."

"I can't believe you're tracking me!"

"And I can't believe you're worried about me tracking you when you're likely facing murder charges."

"Murder? What are you talking about?"

"What your father is trying to say, is that the GPS data makes you the primary suspect," Hitchens said.

Abbott walked in and whispered to Hitchens, then showed him a piece of evidence in a plastic bag.

"R.V. can you come in here?" Hitchens asked.

R.V. walked into the living room and sat. "What do y'all need?"

"We checked with the clerk," Abbott said.

"And if you checked, I'm sure he told you I was there, buying dip," R.V. said.

"We also looked at the videotape."

Abbott held up the evidence bag. "When we zoomed in, we saw this piece of evidence coming off your shoe. I bet when we get it analyzed, it will show it to be the grass from Ellis's backyard."

"That's bullshit!"

"Mr. Richards, would you dial Shawna's phone, please?" Hitchens asked.

A ringing sound was heard in the foyer.

"I must have left it in my jacket," Shawna said.

Abbott returned smirking. "You did, Shawna. You must have forgotten to take it out when you came back from the Ellis house."

"I wasn't at the Ellis house," Shawna insisted.

Abbott patted her back. "I know you weren't — now, I do. It seems as if R.V. grabbed your jacket by mistake, or on purpose, so he could frame you."

"Are you crazy?" R.V. asked.

"Not a bit R.V. We examined the store's videotape. It clearly shows you wearing Shawna's jacket."

Abbott pointed to a logo on the back of the jacket. "See that? You can see the high school logo on the back. Why did you wear her hoodie to the store?"

Abbott held up the evidence bag when R.V. didn't answer. "You can also see this crucial piece of evidence left on the floor from your shoe."

R.V. scrunched his eyebrows. "Maybe I grabbed the wrong jacket. They're both black."

"Yes, you did, R.V. And you wore it when you killed Mrs. Ellis, which is why Mr. Richard's app shows Shawna's phone at the Ellis house at the time of her murder," Abbott said.

Hitchens leaned forward. "You want to tell us about it?"

Tom burst into the room and grabbed R.V. by the neck. He banged R.V.'s head against the back of the chair. Ron rushed over and punched R.V. in the face repeatedly.

Abbott and Hitchens pulled Ron and Tom off R.V., then R.V. wiped blood from his face while Tom glared at him.

"You killed her for money! For goddamn money? You son of a bitch!" Tom shouted.

"I didn't do anything," R.V. said.

Abbott looked at his notes. "We timed it out, R.V. You had plenty of time to stop at the Ellis house, then get to the bodega. If it weren't for the clerk noticing the high school logo, you might have gotten away with it."

"Good luck proving that," R.V. replied.

"Between the tape showing you wearing the jacket and showing the evidence coming from your shoe, not to mention Ed's tracking app, we've got you nailed," Abbott said.

Ron rushed over and punched R.V. in the face again. "You son of a bitch!"

Hitchens stood, put cuffs on R.V, and led him toward the front door. Tom struggled to restrain Ron as he passed.

"You have the right to remain silent," Hitchens began.

Tom sat there stunned. He kept thinking back to their last conversation that evening. How she'd been upset about the gambling, about the money. He'd never get a chance to tell her he was sorry. He'd never get to show her he could change. All because R.V. wanted his money.

That's what made it worse. Tom knew R.V. needed the cash. He'd been laid off because of Alyssa's consulting work. His kid was in trouble. But to kill Alyssa over it? Twenty thousand dollars wasn't enough to take a life.

As Tom watched them take R.V. away, he felt nothing but rage. Rage at R.V. for killing his wife. Rage at himself for leaving things as they were between them. And rage at the world that would let something like this happen.

They said the evidence was solid. The hoodie. The tracking app. The blade of grass. All of it pointing to R.V. But none of it would bring Alyssa back. None of it would fix what had been broken.

Tom put his arm around Ron, and they stood there, father and son, watching as they led her killer away. Alyssa was gone, but at least they'd have justice. It was a hollow comfort, but it was all they had.

PART FOUR

UNTIL TOMORROW

Until Tomorrow is a poignant, emotionally charged novella about love, loss, and the thin line between holding on and letting go. When Marna Maloney suffers a catastrophic stroke and slips into a locked-in state — aware but unable to move or speak — her husband Tom clings to hope with a daily ritual: a single red rose, bedside stories, and whispered updates from the life she can no longer share.

As he juggles work, mounting bills, and two grieving children desperate to know whether their mother can still hear them, Tom faces the impossible question of how to keep living while the love of his life is trapped between worlds — until one final, uncanny goodbye suggests that some promises last beyond a last heartbeat.

AN EMERGENCY SITUATION

"Code blue! Code blue!"

The urgent announcement echoed through the hallway of Memorial Hospital.

Doctors and nurses rushed into the emergency room where Marna Maloney lay unconscious after collapsing at home during dinner. Her husband, Tom, stood frozen outside the room, watching through the glass as medical staff worked desperately to stabilize her.

"Massive stroke," he overheard a doctor saying. "Get her prepped for surgery immediately."

Tom couldn't breathe. Just an hour ago, they were laughing together as Ethan told a joke from school. Marna served chicken parmesan, their Friday tradition. Then she grabbed her head, made a strange sound, and collapsed. The pasta bowl shattered on the floor.

Eight-year-old Ethan and ten-year-old Judy now sat in the waiting room with their neighbor, Mrs. Peterson, who had come over when she heard the ambulance. Tom called her in a panic, not knowing who else to ask.

"Mr. Maloney?" A surgeon appeared, still putting on his cap. "We need to operate immediately. Your wife suffered a severe hemorrhagic stroke. We'll do everything we can."

"Will she ...?" Tom couldn't finish the sentence.

The surgeon placed a hand on his shoulder. "We'll know more after surgery. The next few hours are critical."

Those few hours turned into a night, which turned into a week in the ICU. Then two weeks. The hemorrhage was stopped, but the damage was extensive.

Marna didn't wake up. Instead, after multiple tests and evaluations, the neurologist delivered the devastating news.

"She's in what we call a "locked-in' state," he said gently. "Her brain stem was severely affected by the stroke. She's conscious and aware, but paralyzed — unable to move or speak. Only her eyes retain some function, though that's limited as well."

"But she'll recover?" Tom asked.

The doctor's hesitation said everything. "Some patients show improvement over time, but I must be honest — her case is severe. We'll continue with treatments and therapies, but you should prepare yourselves."

Three months later, Tom's life had become an exhausting routine. Work, children, hospital visits, bills — repeat. Every day, he brought Marna a single red rose, replacing the previous day's flower that, inevitably, was wilted.

Tom Maloney climbed the steps to St. Luke's Hospital slowly, holding the handrail for support. Marna was transferred here two weeks ago for long-term care.

His breathing became labored as he reached the fourth floor. The single red rose in his hand was a daily ritual, a promise he made to himself and to Marna.

The long hallway to room #474 seemed to stretch endlessly. He'd walked this path so many times he could trace it blindfolded.

When he entered the room, Marna lay motionless in the hospital bed. Her eyes were wide open, but her gaze was empty, devoid of life. She was locked-in — completely paralyzed, unable to speak or move, but fully conscious and aware of her surroundings. At least that's what they told him. Some days he believed it, others he wasn't so sure.

Tom crossed the room and replaced yesterday's rose with the fresh one. The dim fluorescent lights cast a sterile glow throughout the room, and the steady beep of a heart monitor echoed in the silence. As he neared the bed, the monitor displayed an increase in heart rate.

For a moment — a short one — Tom was filled with excitement. He turned to Nurse Debbie, sitting comfortably in a chair against the wall, but she shook her head.

"The heart rate varies, Tom. We don't know why, but it does."

"I thought —"

Debbie stepped over and held his hand. "There's been no change yet ... but that doesn't mean there won't be. The neurologist was here yesterday, and based on Marna's responsiveness to the EEG, he feels she is in a "locked-in" state, not a coma.

"I wouldn't get too optimistic, but I definitely wouldn't give up hope."

Tom pulled a chair next to her bed and sat to read a book.

"I know this isn't an adult book, but the kids loved it so much when you read it to them: I'll teach my dog 100 words ..."

As he read, Tom studied Marna's face, searching for any sign that she heard him. Her beauty remained, even now, beneath the stillness. He wondered if she could hear him, if she knew how much he missed her voice, her touch, her laugh.

"Will she ever recover?" he asked, standing and walking toward Debbie. "Will she ever be able to speak? To move?"

Debbie gently took his hands and lowered her head. "I don't know if she'll get better, but she might. Regardless, we'll keep her as comfortable as possible."

Tom swallowed hard, feeling the familiar tightness in his throat.

"Tom, I couldn't help overhearing your call about missing work,"

Debbie said. "You don't have to come every day. I'll even sit with her during lunch if you want me to."

His face contorted in shock. "But she'll miss me."

"I doubt she knows the days. Why not come two or three times a week?"

"I'll consider it," he said, but the thought crushed him.

Tom stared at Debbie, his lips slightly parted. He looked down, thinking. "On second thought, I'll be back tomorrow."

He stopped at the door, then turned back. "Are you certain she can't hear me? Can't see me?"

Nurse Debbie hesitated, then nodded solemnly. "I'm sorry, Tom. I just don't know. The doctors don't either."

Just then, Tom noticed something. Marna's face ... did it change? "She smiled! I saw her smile."

The nurse walked to Marna and looked closely at her. She tapped Marna's arm but saw no response. She looked at the monitor, and though it showed a small increase in heart rate, it was almost negligible. She turned back to Tom.

"That could have been an involuntary muscle contraction. But whatever it was, it's not there now."

Tom lowered his head and sobbed. "I'm leaving, Marna. I've got to get to work."

His footsteps echoed in the emptiness of the stairwell as he left.

HOW TO CONTINUE

At International Solutions, Tom exited the elevator, looked at the time, and rushed toward his desk. As he took his seat, his boss turned the corner and pulled a rolling chair beside him.

"Tom, I know Marna's stroke was a shock. I can't even imagine ... but we've gone to great lengths to accommodate you. I just can't have you coming in late every day."

Tom nodded. "I'll do better, I'll even put in extra hours on the weekend if I have to."

"Never mind that. Just get here on time from now on." His boss got up to leave, then turned. "And take off early today. Spend time with the kids."

At home, Tom sat at the kitchen table, his computer screen filled with spreadsheets showing bills that were due. He shook his head, muttering, "How the hell am I gonna pay these?"

The front door opened, and Judy and Ethan ran to him and wrapped their arms around him.

"Daddy! You're home," Judy said.

Ethan threw his arms around Tom. "Daddy!"

Tom scooped them both up in his arms, hugged, and kissed them.

"I missed you so much. It's been almost … a day since I've seen you."

The kids laughed and jumped down.

"Can we play games or go to the park?" Judy asked.

"It will have to be another day, guys. I have to finish paying bills, and then do some work."

"Yuk. Do I have to do work when I grow up?" Ethan asked.

Judy laughed. "Of course, silly. Everybody works."

The next day, Tom replaced the rose by Marna's bed, then sat and chatted.

"The kids were in a great mood last night. They miss you a lot. And Ethan has grown so much. He's almost as tall as Judy now, but thankfully not as sassy."

Marna didn't move, didn't smile, or even blink. Tom read a chapter from *The Mayor of Casterbridge*, another one of her favorites, then he set it down gently and kissed her lips.

"I just stopped by to say 'hi,' but I really need to go. I can't afford to be late for work again."

The wind howled as the heavy door slammed shut behind him. Tom didn't flinch. His breath fogged in the cold air, but he didn't seem to notice. As he walked toward the parking lot, slow but deliberate, his shoes crunched softly against gravel and patches of ice.

"It's not right," he muttered to himself.

He stopped near the car, leaned against the hood, and looked up. The sky was overcast, fitting the day perfectly.

Tom reached for his keys and brought out a few wilted petals from the red rose. It brought a smile.

"She'd say I should have brought tulips," he said to himself.

A gust of wind ripped through the open parking lot. Tom shivered and got in the car.

"I'll be back tomorrow," he said softly.

He opened the car door and got in, but didn't start the engine right away. He just sat and held the steering wheel.

That night, at Tom's house, a soft lamp glowed in the corner of the living room, illuminating a game board spread across the floor. It was surrounded by snacks and scattered cards.

Tom sat cross-legged with Judy and Ethan. They laughed as Ethan moved the wrong piece across the board.

"Ethan! That's not even your piece."

"I always play with the green one," he said.

Judy laughed loudly, slapping her hands on the floor. "That's the brown piece, Ethan."

They collapsed into laughter, a welcome change in the house. And even though the sound felt strange — new, maybe even forced — it was a sound they all needed. One that was missing for too long.

Ethan crossed the finish with his last roll of the dice. He jumped up and down, shouting, "I win. I win."

"All right, rascals. Time for bed."

The kids groaned in unison, and Judy tugged his sleeve. "Did you see Mommy today? You didn't tell us how she was."

Ethan ran over, suddenly serious. "Did she ask about me? Did she talk? Or do anything?"

Tom crouched, arms wide. They rushed into his embrace, and he held them tightly, longer than usual.

"I *did* see her, but she didn't talk. Maybe tomorrow. I'll let you know. And I promise, as soon as the doctors tell me Mommy can hear you, or as soon as she talks, I'm taking you in to see her — even if I have to take you out of school to do it."

"For real?" Ethan asked.

"It's a promise." Tom kissed the tops of their heads, then slowly released them. "Come on, let's get you upstairs."

Tom walked them up the stairs, one hand on Judy's shoulder, the other holding Ethan's tiny fingers.

"Can she still dream?" Ethan asked.

Tom paused halfway up the stairs, taken off guard, but he made sure not to cry. "I don't know, buddy. I hope so."

"Maybe she dreams about us?" Judy wondered.

"Mostly me, though," Ethan added.

Tom smiled, but it was pained. He nodded, eyes misting. "I'm sure she dreams about both of you."

They reached the top. Tom flipped the hallway light on, casting light over framed photos: Marna with the kids, Marna and Tom in Italy, and another picture showing Marna dancing barefoot in the kitchen.

He stared at the pictures — maybe for too long.

Tom tucked Judy in, then Ethan. He sat on the edge of the bed for a moment, brushing Ethan's hair back.

"We need to get this mop of yours cut, or at least trimmed."

Ethan shook his head, then held up a family drawing. "Tell Mommy I drew her a picture," he said sleepily.

"I will."

Tom stopped by Judy's room, who was already curled up under her blanket, staring at the ceiling.

"Does she still remember my favorite color?" she asked.

Tom froze. "I'll be sure to remind her. It's orange, right?"

Judy playfully slapped his arm. "You know it's purple."

Tom kissed her forehead and turned off the light. As he closed the door behind him, Judy called out, "Tell her we love her."

"Every day," he promised.

Tom entered his room slowly, his shoulders slumped. He closed the door behind him without turning on the light, then sat on the edge of the bed. The room was lit only by moonlight filtering through the curtains.

He flopped on his side of the bed and reached over to an empty pile of blankets and two pillows. After lying down, he stared at the ceiling. His breath caught as he squeezed his eyes shut.

"Don't cry. The kids might hear," he whispered to himself.

He curled slightly onto his side, and a single sob escaped before he buried his face in the pillow.

Morning light spilled across the kitchen counter as Tom stood at the stove, flipping pancakes. A small radio played softly in the background — cheerful music that didn't match how he felt. Eggs sizzled. Toast popped up, and he moved like a machine — present, but not really there.

The kids sat at the table, still in pajamas. Ethan cut up a pancake with too much syrup, a sneer on his face. And Judy stared into her orange juice.

"What's wrong with your juice?" Tom asked.

"Mommy always strained my orange juice. I don't like the stringy things in there."

Tom smiled — a genuine smile. "I'll make sure to do better."

"Tell her we said hi," Judy said.

"I will."

Ethan grabbed his backpack and headed for the door. "And tell her we love her and miss her! Especially her breakfast."

"Are you going to school in your pajamas?"

Ethan laughed, tossed his backpack on the floor, then ran upstairs to dress. Judy was already on her way down.

Moments later, they both raced out the door.

Tom wiped his eyes quickly with the back of his hand, then forced a smile. He shouted to the kids as the door closed. "I'll tell her everything."

The door closed, and Tom exhaled. His hands trembled as he poured himself a cup of coffee. He took a sip, then glanced upstairs.

The hum of the refrigerator was the only sound in the room. He looked down at his shirt and noticed a syrup stain from Ethan's hug. It produced another genuine smile, the second of the day.

Tom dropped the car off at the shop to get repaired, then took a cab to the hospital.

He climbed the stairs, slower than usual. His knees ached and his breath was shallow, but he kept going, each step an echo. As he reached the fourth floor, he glanced up — and froze as the intercom crackled.

"Code blue! Room 474 — code blue!"

Several doctors in white coats rushed down the hall and into Marna's room. Nurses and aides gathered outside.

"That's Marna's room!" Tom said in panic.

He quickened his pace, dropping the rose as he ran.

When he entered, Nurse Debbie grabbed his arm and pulled him aside. "You'll have to wait, Tom. The doctors are with her now."

Tom tensed as the heart monitor beeped wildly.

Defibrillator paddles were prepped and placed on her chest. Her cardiologist spoke loudly.

"Clear!"

A jolt shook Marna's body, then again. The monitor flatlined. There was a buzz of activity as a sense of panic filled the air.

Tom breathed deeply and held it as he stared and waited.

"Again. Clear!" Another jolt. Nothing.

"One more time. Clear!"

Still nothing. The doctors stepped away, casting defeated looks to each other. The cardiologist gave a loud sigh and looked at the clock.

Just then, a low beep was heard, and when the doctor looked, a few blips showed on the monitor. Then more.

Tom let out a huge sigh and wept openly. He walked toward her, but Debbie stopped him.

"The doctors need to work," she whispered.

"Just one minute? Please?"

Debbie looked to the cardiologist, who nodded.

Tom moved closer, leaned down and kissed her cheek. "Don't worry, I'll be with you again someday."

Something strange happened then. Tom could swear he heard her voice, as clear as day, though her lips didn't move: "My sweet darling, it's time for me to go. We've had a wonderful life together, and all I want is for you to be happy and give the same love you gave me to the kids. I'll be waiting for you. Love you always."

Nurse Debbie softly held his hand and led him to the door. "Marna's probably exhausted, Tom. And I'm sure the doctors will need to keep a close watch on her."

Tom nodded, almost unconsciously, then jumped up, a panicked look on his face. "I forgot about the kids. They get off early today."

He ran down the hallway, his heels echoing loudly, then down the stairs until he got outside.

As Tom stepped onto the sidewalk, a gentle breeze brushed him, causing a shiver. He shook his head as if to clear it, then shook it again.

The wind swirled around him, rustling leaves. He listened to the sounds that calmed him and thought to himself, "I swear I heard her voice, almost like she whispered in my ear."

He shrugged and buttoned his coat, then fastened his collar. Tom continued on his way, but there was a new bounce to his step.

A passerby tipped his hat. "Looks like you're having a good day."

Tom smiled. "I am, thank you. Better than most."

He exhaled. His breath lingered in the air, and for the first time in months, he felt ... warm. As he continued down the street, a cabbie pulled over and rolled down the window.

"Hey, pal. Want a ride?"

Tom smiled and shook his head. "It's a nice day. I think I'll walk."

The cabbie looked at him in amazement. "You're nuts."

Tom laughed, then glanced at the clock on the bank across the street. "Shit! Eleven o'clock," he said aloud.

He looked back to the cabbie, who was just pulling from the curb. Tom whistled loudly, causing him to stop.

"On second thought, I'll take that ride. I've got to pick my kids up at noon. Take me to St. Catherine's and wait. I'll only be a minute, then we can go to my house; it's only a few blocks from there."

Tom stood tall at St. Catherine's and rubbed his hands together to keep warm. When he saw the kids coming, he knelt down and spread his arms wide, embracing them in a big hug.

"You're happy today. Is Mommy better?" Judy asked.

"Not yet, but maybe getting there."

They all got in the cab and headed home.

As they entered the house, the phone rang.

"Mr. Maloney, this is Debbie from St. Luke's. I'm so sorry ... but Marna passed. It was only a few moments after you left. If it makes a difference, the time of death was 10:58."

Tom stared blankly at the wall and lowered the receiver slowly. He set it on the hook, then he thought back.

"That was when I was leaving. When I heard her voice. I think she said goodbye."

In that moment, Tom knew that even though she was gone, she would always be with them. In the kids' smiles, in the memories they made, and in the love that would never fade. *Until tomorrow, my love. Until we meet again.*

PART FIVE

THE JURY

In this high-stakes psychological thriller, a group of strangers are lured to a remote island for a mysterious weekend retreat — soon discovering they've been selected to serve as jurors in a perilous, real-life trial where the fate of an accused criminal hangs in their hands.

As the group confronts evidence, secrets, and moral dilemmas, trust dissolves and motives clash. But the ordeal isn't over: each must vote on the fate of their fellow jurors, and not everyone will leave alive.

Intense and suspenseful, the story asks — what is justice when everyone is guilty?

THE PLAN

Alphonse sat at a street-side table outside a quaint café in Paris, staring absently at his espresso. The morning air was crisp, and pedestrians hurried past, paying no attention to him, which was fine. He preferred anonymity.

A woman approached, and sat across from him. She lit a cigarette, crossed her legs, then flipped her hair, and stared.

"Bonjour, Monsieur," she said. "*Je m'appelle* Juliette."

"Speak English or don't speak," Alphonse said, more gruffly than he intended.

She continued in perfect English. "My name is Juliette," she said, then took a sip of her coffee, and looked up at him thoughtfully.

"I know who you are, and I know what happened to your family. I've seen that look in your eyes before — in others. If I were you, I would consider options, ones that will make you happy."

She leaned closer to him. "My friend suffered with a similar situation, and looked only for vengeance. When an alternative was presented, she listened, and are much more content now."

"What the hell would you know?"

Juliette uncrossed her legs, leaned forward, and lowered her voice. "When I said I'd seen that look before, it was when *I* looked in the mirror. I lost everything — my husband *and* my three children. A drunk driver ran into them as they drove home from a soccer game."

Juliette sat up straight and lit another cigarette. "And the drunken fool who did it served no time and got no punishment. All because he had wealthy friends. So when I say I know what you're going through, I do."

Alphonse folded his hands on the table in front of him. He stared with renewed interest. "What did you do?"

"I got even the only way I could. I found out everything about his business dealings, all the bribes and payoffs, the money laundering, and more. Then, I had some friends in the newspaper business publish these findings." She sipped her espresso, draining the cup. "He never went to prison, but we ruined his life. It was a minor form of vengeance."

"And you think I should go this route?"

"You could listen."

After a moment of silence, Juliette said, "Would you like to hear about it?"

Alphonse sighed. "It doesn't hurt to listen."

RECRUITING THE TALENT

Days later, Alphonse was in New York. Buildings towered overhead as business men and women hurried along the sidewalk, half with phones pressed against their ears. He spotted his target immediately.

Rhonda Crenshaw strutted down a bustling sidewalk, weaving through a crowd of people. She clutched her Birkin bag and suspiciously scanned everyone she passed. Alphonse approached her as she waited for the signal to change. He tipped his hat to her and bowed.

"Good morning, Madam. Would you care to join me for a cup of coffee?"

"I don't know you," she said, annoyed.

Alphonse laughed and put his hat back on.

"But I know you, Rhonda, and I have a proposition I believe you'll find of interest. In fact, knowing your penchant for finding new ways to make money, I'm sure you will."

Rhonda tucked in her scarf and shot him a sideways glance. She looked up at the skyscrapers surrounding her, took off her gloves, and looked straight ahead, ignoring him.

"Well?"

The morning sun reflected off the mirrored glass buildings creating a near-blinding light. Rhonda pointed to a small café, fifty yards away.

"I *am* hungry but I've got places to be, so it can't take long."

Alphonse gave her a wry smile. "In a hurry to make more money?"

Inside the coffee shop, they sat at a window table and ordered coffee and a bagel. Steam rose from the cup as Rhonda wrapped her hands around it for warmth. She sipped slowly, checked the time, then looked at him.

"All right, we're here."

"I would like you to join a few others for a weekend retreat on my island. Expenses are paid, and you'll want for nothing."

Rhonda offered a thin smile. "I don't want, or need, a retreat."

"I understand. Pushing penny stocks and running Ponzi schemes takes a lot of effort."

Her head snapped backward, and she narrowed her eyes. "I have nothing to do with Ponzi schemes."

Alphonse chuckled. "All right. For the sake of argument, let's assume you have nothing to do with Ponzi schemes."

"Why me?" she asked.

"You will be told everything once we arrive."

"And this is nothing illegal?"

"Would it make a difference?"

"I don't like evasive answers, and I want a guarantee."

"Life has no guarantees. Besides, who else pays you to take a vacation?"

"How do I know you'll keep your word about getting paid?"

"You will be paid $1 million — $250k when you arrive at the airstrip and the rest upon returning."

Rhonda took a big gulp of her coffee while Alphonse glanced at his watch, then stared at her.

"Business can wait; this can't."

Rhonda looked over the rim of the cup as she finished her coffee, then she leaned back and put on her gloves.

"And you're sure this isn't illegal?"

"No more so than a Ponzi scheme."

"All right. Count me in."

Alphonse jotted down an address on the back of a napkin. "Be there by six on Friday."

He stood, laid a fifty-dollar bill on the table, and then exited, walking casually down the street.

Harris McKenna waited outside a bank, meticulously dressed and carrying a briefcase. He continually checked the time flashing on a billboard across the street. It appeared as if he was waiting for the bank to open. Alphonse stepped beside him, flashed a disarming smile, and extended his hand.

"Alphonse Falcone. Would you care to join me for a cup of coffee? I have a proposition I believe you'll find of interest."

Harris looked around, left to right. "I'm waiting for the bank to open."

"The bank doesn't open for twenty minutes. We should be finished long before then."

Alphonse repeated the process with his other prospects.

He approached Amanda Chen while she spoke on the phone, covering her ear with her hand to block out the noise of the traffic.

And finally, he walked up behind Robert Calhoun, introduced himself, and invited him for lunch, indicating he had a deal that he should listen to.

Friday Night

Alphonse's private jet sat ready on the tarmac. Four passengers boarded, impressed by what greeted them: plush leather seats on each side of a wide aisle, which led to a full spacious bathroom, wood paneling, mood lighting, large windows, and a fully equipped kitchen.

As they walked down the aisle, they passed a conference room. At the end sat a private bedroom suite. As the passengers took their seats, Alphonse emerged from the bedroom, perfectly dressed.

"Welcome aboard," he said. "Before we begin, enter your routing number, and I'll send the initial deposit."

He handed each person a tablet and a menu, then returned to his bedroom.

"Just tell the chef your preference."

Once he was gone, Rhonda reached across the aisle and introduced herself to Harris.

"I'm Rhonda Crenshaw. You have any idea what the hell we're doing here?"

Harris shook Rhonda's hand. "Harris McKenna, VP at ULC HealthCare. I don't know why we're here, but he offered good money."

Rhonda pushed her long auburn hair behind her ear and twirled it with her finger. She then looked at Harris and nodded.

"I've done some crazy things before, but this seems edgy."

Robert jiggled change in his pocket as he walked down the aisle. He winked at Rhonda, and tapped Harris' arm.

"I just talked to Amanda but she knows nothing. Looks like we're all in the dark."

Amanda returned from the bar holding two glasses of wine, and biting her lip. She gestured toward Harris' seat.

"Mind if I sit there? I want to speak to Rhonda."

Harris stood, and walked up the aisle, Robert behind him. Rhonda looked over at Amanda.

"What do you need?"

Amanda leaned toward her and whispered. "I didn't want anything. That guy just gives me the creeps."

Rhonda's eyes opened wide. "I got the same vibes."

Nine hours later, the sun peeked through a window with an open shutter, a shocking wake-up call. Harris swallowed hard, trying to clear the pressure building in his ears. Rhonda checked her phone while Robert sipped champagne and smoked a cigarette.

Amanda brushed her hand in the air. "Put that damn thing out, please."

The pilot made an announcement. His deep voice crackled over the intercom.

"Ladies and gentlemen, we are beginning our descent to Falcone Island. Please buckle up."

THE ISLAND

The jet touched down on a small airstrip carved into a lush tropical landscape. As the passengers disembarked, Rhonda took a deep breath and admired the surroundings.

Robert took off his jacket and draped it over his shoulder as he looked around. "Don't tell Alphonse, but I'd have come here for nothing."

"It is a bit nicer than what we left," Amanda said.

Alphonse climbed into a sleek black limo which waited nearby, and the others joined him. The limo moved along an ocean-front road, the waves crashing against jagged rocks far below.

At the first intersection, the driver turned up a steep incline until he reached a three-story mansion atop a plateau. He parked under a large overhang, stepped out of the limo, and showed them into the house.

They entered a massive foyer with marble floors, wood-paneled walls, and spiral staircases on each side. The silence was deafening as everyone looked around.

"If we're being held hostage, I could think of a worse place," Amanda said.

Frederick, Alphonse's butler, stepped into the foyer and greeted them. "If you will follow me, please? Mr. Falcone will join us shortly."

The group entered a library with floor-to-ceiling shelves of leather-bound books. Alphonse was already seated in a high-back leather chair. He gestured for them to sit.

"Before we begin, please surrender cell phones and/or tablets. They will be returned when you leave."

Robert shook his head. "I don't give my phone to anyone."

"They'll be returned. I just cannot allow outside communications."

The rest of the group handed over their phones, but Robert refused to surrender his. Alphonse moved in front of Robert.

"Turn over the phone, or go home with no further payment."

Robert reluctantly handed his phone to Frederick, while glaring at Alphonse. Frederick then got them drinks.

"I'm sure you're wondering why I asked you here," Alphonse said.

"I need to be back by Sunday night," Amanda said.

"Do your job, and you will be."

Robert took a long sip of his coffee and set the cup on the table, letting it hit hard. "And what the hell is our job?"

"You are here as jurors, and you —"

"Jurors?" Harris asked.

"Let me finish, Harris." Alphonse paused. "You will decide the fate of a man who has done unspeakable crimes, but the justice system has set him free. If, after hearing the evidence, you are inclined to set him free, so be it. If not, he'll be sentenced to death."

"Are you crazy? I won't be responsible for a man's death," Amanda said.

"If you think he's innocent — vote 'not guilty.' But the vote must be unanimous. Four 'not guilty' votes, or four 'guilty' votes."

"And if we don't agree?" Amanda asked.

"No one leaves the island until we get a unanimous verdict. I'll allow a few moments for you to consider this."

Robert paced, jiggling his change as he evaluated the others.

Amanda stared suspiciously as she chewed on her nails.

Harris arranged the bills in his money clip, making them all face one way.

Rhonda sat still and hummed continuously.

"For Christ's sake, stop the humming. It's driving me crazy," Robert said.

Alphonse rang a bell that sat on a table next to him. "Let's freshen up. We'll reconvene in one hour?"

One hour later, chairs were arranged in a semi-circle. Each chair had a name tag hung on the back of it. Alphonse sat on a large cushioned sofa, pulled out a pipe, and lit it.

"While you are here, following instructions is paramount."

The jurors exchanged glances. A few narrowed their eyes.

"You have been chosen as jurors of a master criminal. Your decisions will shape the future, not only for him, but others as well."

"What the hell have I gotten into?" Amanda muttered to herself.

With brows furrowed and mouths slightly agape, the jurors shifted uncomfortably in their seats, hands gripping the edges of their armrests. Rhonda nervously tapped a pen against the table, while Harris wiped a bead of sweat from his forehead, and Amanda chewed her nails. The room was silent, save for the soft rustle of clothing and the occasional sharp intake of breath, as if everyone were holding back a collective exhale.

Harris leaned close to Robert and whispered. "I don't like this."

Alphonse watched closely, his expression unreadable.

"The man on trial is accused of molesting an eight-year-old girl. In addition, he beat to death a young man who witnessed his crime. Read the transcript of the trial and decide on his guilt or innocence. You may ask him questions, but please keep them to a minimum."

The jurors looked at each other in disbelief. Alphonse remained impassive, awaiting their reactions with an unnerving smile.

"What the hell? No way. Not me," Robert said.

Alphonse gave a dismissive laugh. "Mr. Calhoun, surely you're not telling me your manipulation of insurance rates has not affected people's lives?"

"I didn't —"

Alphonse lowered his tone, and leaned forward. "I have the data, Mr. Calhoun."

The atmosphere grew charged as the reality of the situation sank in. Frederick poured more wine into their glasses, to ease the tension.

Alphonse stared. "We're here for the weekend, so please, try to relax. This will be an enlightening, and possibly rewarding, experience."

Amanda bit her lip and opened her notepad. "Why us? And why here?"

"And where the hell are we?" Robert asked.

"You are on my island, and you have been selected for your unique perspectives. Each of you have committed crimes and have gotten away with them — so far."

Robert sat up straight and lit a cigarette. Then he leaned back and blew a cloud of smoke into the air.

"The others might be criminals, but I haven't done a damn thing."

"Really?" Alphonse said. "We've already been through your activities. Don't make me list them again."

"What if we refuse?" Robert interrupted.

"Refusal is not an option — unless you want specifics of what you do to appear in all the papers, and spread all over social media."

"You said the man already received his trial. Why do it again?"

Alphonse shifted in his seat and rested his arm on the edge of the sofa. He pulled a pipe from his jacket and re-lit it.

"Let's put an end to this now. All of you have done things that could, and should, land you in prison. Rhonda, you've run Ponzi schemes and pushed worthless stocks to make money, among other crimes. Do your job right, and your activities won't be made public."

Alphonse gestured toward an ornate door at the far end of the room. He stood and headed toward it. "Follow me and we will begin."

The jurors followed, brows furrowed and eyes wide open. They whispered among themselves as they walked down the intricately decorated hallway, the walls adorned with unsettling paintings. Amanda leaned forward and tapped Harris' arm.

"What have we gotten involved with?"

Harris looked side to side and shook his head. "I don't like it."

Alphonse led them into a room that opened to a dimly lit chamber. A long, rectangular table sat in the center with an iPad, and folders filled with legal documents, sitting before each juror's seat. The walls were barren, save for a large monitor mounted above a fireplace.

Amanda shivered and chewed her lip as she and the other jurors sat, and looked around cautiously. Alphonse stepped in front of the fireplace and cleared his voice loudly.

"Please be patient. The defendant will be introduced momentarily."

Alphonse stepped back and faced the monitor, then pressed the remote. The monitor flickered and a man appeared on the monitor. He sat at a table, sweat beading on his forehead.

"The man you're about to judge will live or die, depending on you, so consider your vote carefully."

The screen focused on the man, casting a cold glow across the room and revealing the silhouette of Josh Brecklin, head shaved, glasses, cloaked in shadows.

Rhonda gasped, and Robert sat up straight, choking on the smoke from his cigarette. The tension was palpable.

"The prisoner is charged with child molestation and murder."

Alphonse paused the monitor and addressed the jurors.

"It is your job to review the transcript of the original trial. I assure you, the process will be fair and respectful. The folders contain all the evidence you need."

Alphonse clicked the monitor on, and headed toward the exit. He grabbed the door handle, but turned to face the jurors.

"I forgot to mention that all votes will be confidential and should be entered into the tablet before you. Discussion of the case is now permitted; in fact, discussion is encouraged."

Alphonse exited, leaving the jurors to themselves. They studied the data in the folders, then argued about evidence among themselves, and they posed questions to the defendant.

Amanda went first. "Your DNA was found under her nails, and in her vagina. Explain that."

"Someone must have planted it," Josh said.

"What about the witness?" Robert asked. "He also had your DNA under his nails."

Josh shook his head. "I'm telling you, I did nothing."

The questions continued for hours, with each juror pressing the defendant for answers that never seemed to satisfy.

"Explain — or try to — why anyone's DNA would be found on a molested child's body, let alone inside her body," Rhonda said, jabbing a pen onto the paper in front of her.

"And how did the witness — who wasn't familiar with you previously — pick you out of a lineup?" Harris glared at Josh's image on the monitor.

"I give everyone the benefit of the doubt, but you aren't helping. Give us something to go on. Anything," Robert said, pausing while Josh drank a glass of water.

Amanda shook her head, indicating she had no questions.

Hours later, Rhonda sighed. "It's been hours. I say we call it quits and vote."

Robert tilted his head back and nodded. "He's guilty as sin."

"Votes are supposedly confidential," Amanda said.

Robert looked around. "If I'm voting on a man's life, I'm going to need more coffee. How the hell do we get that?"

Harris sighed and shook his head. "Great, a caffeine-addicted juror."

"I didn't hear you get any gold stars from the man, so shut up."

Harris pressed a button, and Frederick poked his head inside.

"How may I help?"

"I want a coffee — black, and piping hot. Make sure it's piping hot," Robert said.

A loud click was heard as Frederick closed the door.

"This is creepy as shit. I can't wait to get out of here," Robert said.

"Alphonse said we can leave after we vote," Amanda said.

Amanda, Robert, and Harris entered their votes on the iPad.

"It doesn't matter how we vote as long as the vote is unanimous," Harris said.

"Don't try to influence the vote. We can decide on our own," Rhonda countered.

The jurors leaned over their tablets and entered their votes. Once done, they pressed the button to call Frederick, who entered almost instantaneously.

"Alphonse will be here momentarily," Frederick announced.

Alphonse stepped in, smiling, his demeanor confident as always. Frederick gathered the tablets and counted the votes. He signaled Alphonse when he was done.

"A unanimous decision, sir — guilty."

Alphonse smiled. "You've done an excellent job, but before we celebrate, let's conclude our business."

Harris scowled. "An excellent job? Celebrate? What kind of lunatic are you? We just condemned a man to death."

Robert gulped the last of his wine, and sneered at Harris.

"You're right, Mr. McKenna — you condemned a man to death. You voted guilty, didn't you?"

"Yes, but —"

Alphonse rapped his knuckles on the table. "Let's conclude this before dinner."

The monitor's screen flashed on and showed Josh standing on a gallows with a thick rope around his neck. Rhonda gasped, as did Harris. Robert pulled another cigarette from his pack, then realized he was already smoking one.

"I didn't expect to watch him die," Robert said.

"I didn't do it. I swear," Josh said, almost begging.

Before anyone said another word, the trap door opened, and Josh fell, the rope snapping his neck. His feet dangled, and as his body succumbed to oxygen deprivation, spasms occurred in his legs and arms, and he foamed at the mouth.

Rhonda covered her eyes with her hands and turned her head. "Oh, my God! Oh, my God."

Alphonse turned off the monitor. "Disgusting or not, you found him guilty. Dinner will be served momentarily."

THE JURORS

I led them to the dining room. A large table was set with exquisite china and the finest crystal. Four stiff-backed chairs surrounded the table.

The clinking of fine silverware, and the soft murmurs of Frederick and his staff filled the room. Each juror's preferred drink sat on the table in front of their seats.

I stood, addressing the jurors with authority. "Do as you like for the rest of the evening. Breakfast will be at six."

Robert checked the door only to find it locked. Frustrated, he returned to his seat.

"It seems like we're stuck. I just want to get my money and go home."

The conversation shifted, tension hanging in the air.

"Is money all you think about?" Harris asked.

"We sent a man to his death," Amanda said. "Let's think about that. It's one thing to con someone, but this …"

Rhonda hung her head, wrestling with her emotions. "I already regret voting. I should —"

"Should have voted 'not guilty'? Do you really think he was not guilty?" Robert asked.

"Not necessarily, but —"

"Then you voted correctly."

Rhonda blew her nose and wiped her eyes, feeling the weight of their decision. She hummed an old 60s song, then stopped. "I'm going to bed. Alphonse said they'd wake us early."

The jurors pushed back the chairs from the dining table, their movements slow and deliberate. Conversations dwindled to silence as they exited the dining room, and their footsteps echoed softly as they ascended the creaking staircase. One by one, they disappeared down the dimly lit hallway and into their rooms.

The next morning, Frederick went to each juror's door and knocked gently. "Breakfast is ready. Rise and shine."

The jurors took seats at the table and eagerly sipped their beverages while waiting for breakfast.

Robert waited until Frederick came by. "How many times do I have to tell you? I want my coffee piping hot. This is lukewarm, at best."

"I'll get a new cup right away, sir."

"When are we leaving?" Harris asked.

Rhonda twirled her hair and stared at the other jurors.

"Suppose he had a family?" Amanda wondered.

"He should have thought of them before he raped the girl, or killed the kid. He got what was coming," Robert said.

Alphonse stood at the head of the table, his voice resonating through the room.

"We aren't quite finished."

Robert threw his napkin on the table and stood. "What the hell do you mean — not finished? You said all we had to do was judge that criminal."

"I said that you were chosen to judge a criminal. I did not say that was all you had to do."

Frederick returned and placed a tablet in front of each juror. The room grew ominously silent, and Alphonse's voice deepened. It sounded foreboding.

"As I mentioned, each of you has committed serious crimes. The folders before you contain evidence on each juror. You must decide which of you needs to die, and which of you will live. The voting will continue until only two of you remain. Those two will be allowed to leave the island."

Robert jumped up and ran to the door. He tried opening it, but it was locked. He turned and shouted at Alphonse.

"You're fucking nuts. I want out of here now. Right now!"

Frederick calmly approached Robert, pulled out a taser and gave him a minor jolt. Robert collapsed to the floor, convulsing.

Alphonse gestured to Frederick, who picked him up, brought him to the table, and set him in his chair.

"All are guilty of various crimes: pump-and-dumps, denying claims on medical insurance, bilking people on auto insurance, faking clinical trials, and more."

"This is bullshit!" Robert shouted.

"Not to worry, Mr. Calhoun. If you are one of the two remaining when the voting is complete, you will be safely escorted off the island."

Harris pushed his drink to the side. "This is goddamn crazy. I'm not doing it. No way."

"You will all vote, and if you elect not to participate, you will be considered guilty."

Alphonse checked the time. "You have four hours to arrive at a verdict. The folders in front of you contain the evidence required. You each get to cast two votes. Anyone who gets two votes cast against them is guilty."

Alphonse exited the room, leaving the jurors to their decisions. After a moment of hesitation, each one grabbed a folder and began reading.

Rhonda placed her folder on the table and wiped her brow. She seemed haunted by memories of a courtroom two years prior, where she had been questioned about perjury. Sweat beaded on her forehead and her voice had faltered as she answered.

"I'm through with this. If I'm voted guilty, so be it," she said.

Robert pushed his folder to the side. "I'd like to side with you, Rhonda but ... I know who I'm voting for."

He then turned to Harris. "You ready?"

Harris too seemed to be wrestling with memories of his own office, where he had shredded multiple files stamped "DENIED."

Harris cast his vote on the iPad, then looked at Rhonda. "You heard him. If you don't vote, you're guilty. You want to die?"

The rest of the jurors nodded in agreement, then each one cast their vote. When they finished, they called Frederick, who gathered the folders and called Alphonse.

Alphonse walked in, read the reports, looked at the voting records on the tablets, then stood before the jurors.

"Rhonda and Harris, come with me. The rest of you go with Frederick."

Robert pushed his chair back and shoved Frederick aside. "Fuck you twice. I'm not going, and I want off this island."

Alphonse smiled. "I admire your zeal, Mr. Calhoun, but your fate has been decided."

"What the hell's that mean?"

Alphonse smiled grimly, his eyes glinting with menace, then he turned and walked out. Rhonda and Harris followed him.

"Amanda and Robert, if you'll follow me, please?" Frederick said.

Outside the mansion, Rhonda, Harris, and Alphonse got into the limo and headed for the jet that sat on the airstrip.

Rhonda took a seat in the back, leaned forward, and timidly posed a question. "Are we going home?"

"If you mean, do you have to watch them being hanged — you don't."

The driver pulled alongside the jet and opened the doors for them. Afterward, they boarded the jet.

Alphonse sat near the middle of the jet, Rhonda and Harris across from him. As the jet took off, he faced them.

"The two of you have been fortunate enough to survive, however, you may be chosen to participate again, which means your fate remains in question. And if there is a next time, you will have no option. It will depend on how much you change your ways."

Alphonse's smile widened just enough to send an involuntary shiver down the jurors' spines.

"If you are selected again, your folder will contain a notation indicating that it is your second time, which will surely affect the voting. I highly recommend you clean up your acts."

Rhonda and Harris tried to sleep but were awakened when the pilot announced they were about to land.

"Fasten your seat belts, please," the pilot said.

Alphonse sat in a seat close to them. "If you'll provide me with your banking information, I'll deposit the rest of your fee — $750,000."

At the airstrip outside NYC, Harris grabbed his briefcase and almost ran off the jet. Rhonda did the same. Alphonse followed at a leisurely pace, along with the pilot.

"How did this one go?" the pilot asked.

"Both of them seem shaken up enough to change their ways," Alphonse replied.

He watched Rhonda and Harris walk away, and once out of sight, he turned and headed back toward the jet.

"Let's go, my friend. We aren't quite finished."

Back at the mansion, Alphonse stepped into the dining room, where Robert and Amanda were eating, laughing, and drinking.

Robert got up to hug him just as Josh entered the room.

"Good evening, Alphonse," Josh greeted.

"Remarkable how tenacious you are, Josh. Some might say it's hard to keep a good man down."

"It's tough to keep a good man hanged, my friend."

Alphonse smiled and gave Josh a hug.

"Any troubles?" Robert asked.

"None. And they didn't seem eager about the prospect of returning."

"For the right price, I'm always ready to be part of the cast," Amanda said.

"You've done a wonderful job, and you were convincing. Academy Award performances. Remember though, nothing is to be said to anyone or you get no more work."

Alphonse called Frederick to the table.

"Frederick, please transfer the agreed-upon sum to each of our guests' accounts. Gentlemen, I must leave in the morning, but you are welcome to stay as long as you like."

One month later, Harris spotted Rhonda at a corner table in a Wall Street café and headed over. He slid into the seat across from her.

"How've you been?" he asked.

"As good as can be expected. Been busy making my business legit. I'm now focused on helping people."

"Same here. I cut all ties to the past. I have no intention of going back to that damn island."

"Me neither. It creeped me out."

"Maybe we can work together to help people," Harris suggested.

"I'm game. What's on your mind?" Rhonda replied.

Weeks later, Alphonse stood on Wall Street, spotting his new target. Paula Whitley stood on the corner, hailing a cab. She was smartly dressed and wore shades that concealed much of her face.

He approached her, tipped his hat, and bowed.

"Good morning, Madam. Would you care to join me for a cup of coffee?"

ACKNOWLEDGMENTS

It is with great honor that I give eternal gratitude to my wife, all four of my grandkids, and my great-grandson. They give me the inspiration to keep going.

ABOUT THE AUTHOR

Giacomo Giammatteo is the author of gritty crime dramas about murder, mystery, and family. He also writes nonfiction books, including the No Mistakes Careers, No Mistakes Publishing, No Mistakes Grammar, and No Mistakes Writing series.

When Giacomo isn't writing, he's helping his wife take care of the animals in their sanctuary. At last count, they had forty-five — eleven dogs, one horse, six cats, and twenty-six pigs.

Oh, and one crazy — and very large — wild boar, who takes walks with Giacomo every day and also happens to be his best buddy.

nomistakespublishing.com
gg@giacomog.com